DEATH SWIM

Frank and Joe tore down the rocky hill to where the red MG was hidden. In minutes they were crossing a bridge, on their way back to Somerset Village.

Near the end of the bridge a powerful black BMW started to pass them. Dark-tinted windows on the sleek performance car made it impossible to see the driver. The BMW held its position, creeping closer to the MG.

"Watch out!" Joe shouted.

Before Frank could hit the brakes, four thousand pounds of BMW slammed into the side of the little MG. Frank fought to stay on the bridge, but the car spun out of control, jumping over the small curb.

The brothers were tossed forward as the car plummeted down the steep incline toward thirty feet of water.

Books in THE HARDY BOYS CASEFILES® Series

Available from ARCHWAY Paperbacks

THE HARDY BOYS CASEFILES NO. 17

THE NUMBER FILE

FRANKLIN W. DIXON

AN ARCHWAY PAPERBACK
Published by POCKET BOOKS
New York   London   Toronto   Sydney   Tokyo   Singapore

AN ARCHWAY PAPERBACK *Original*

An Archway Paperback published by
POCKET BOOKS, a division of Simon & Schuster Inc.
1230 Avenue of the Americas, New York, NY 10020

ISBN: 0-671-68806-5

First Archway Paperback printing July 1988

10 9 8 7 6 5 4

THE NUMBER FILE

Chapter

1

"JUST ONE SHOT LEFT," Joe Hardy muttered. "I'd better make it count." His blue eyes narrowed in concentration as he sighted along the barrel of his gun. He squeezed the trigger, then his hand whitened on the gun stock. Joe knew he'd missed.

"You're through!" Laughter came from behind Joe, and he turned. His brother, Frank, stood there, grinning in triumph, his teeth bright against his tanned face. "That was your last clay pigeon—I win!"

Frank patted Joe's blond hair, which the early-morning sea breeze had tangled into curls. "Nice aim, Joe," he teased.

Joe shrugged. "My aim was better yesterday—when I shot Kruger."

"There's a big difference between shooting a camera and shooting a gun," Frank answered.

Joe silently agreed and cracked open his shotgun to eject the spent shell. The Hardys had recently found themselves on both sides of guns—being fired at and firing when desperate.

Joe was remembering their last case, *Line of Fire*. They'd both been targets, trying to keep a sharpshooting friend from becoming a murderer.

"Well, this case is a lot easier than that last one," Frank said. "Just observe, take pictures, and enjoy the sun."

Frank and Joe were on the island of Bermuda, in a small town called Somerset Village. They were doing a surveillance job for their famous detective father, Fenton Hardy. For the past few days they'd been staying with an ex-colleague of their dad's, Alfred Montague, and his daughter, Alicia.

Montague, as he preferred to be called, had been a detective with Scotland Yard, and had helped Fenton Hardy with several international cases. He was only too glad to give his friend's sons a base. And he'd been giving the boys some pointers on trap-shooting during their few free hours.

"Want to try another round?" Joe suggested.

Frank glanced at his watch. "We should be heading for Kruger's villa."

"Why? We haven't gotten anything yet," Joe said. "Nothing but a bunch of pictures of Kruger and his house and a tan. If our source was right, in just two days a batch of counterfeit credit cards is going to the U.S. from here. And we have nothing new to tell Dad."

Frank ran a hand through his brown hair. "So you think we'll accomplish more blasting clay pigeons?"

"Well, I'll feel better, beating you."

Frank drew himself up to his full six-one and grinned at his slightly shorter, slightly younger brother. Joe was seventeen. "You're on." Then he turned to wave to the trap house across the carefully tended lawn as Joe reloaded. Montague was inside, running the machinery that would catapult the clay pigeons into the air.

Joe stood seemingly at ease, the shotgun loose in his hands. Frank knew he was tenser than he looked. Joe loved action—and the past few days he'd seen little of it.

Loading his gun, Frank said, "Do you want to take every other shot?" Joe nodded as Frank continued, "At least the stakeout's easy. We sit on a rock under a cedar tree and take pictures of a house by the ocean—"

Joe yelled, "Pull!" The clay pigeon soared

into the sky. Joe's gun rose smoothly to his shoulder, barked, and the clay disk shattered into hundreds of pieces.

"Three shipments with fifteen thousand credit cards already left here," Frank mumbled to himself. "And we only find out about it by accident."

"What did you say?" Joe asked.

"I was just thinking about our source—that counterfeiter who got caught and talked."

"Yeah, if he hadn't supposedly been one of Kruger's couriers, we wouldn't know anything." He smiled, then yelled, "Pull!"

Caught off-guard, Frank jerked up his gun— and missed. He gave Joe a dirty look and added, "Supposedly?"

Joe shrugged. "Well, there's no proof, remember. They only found this guy with the cards made from stolen plates. He rolled over and named Kruger. But we don't have *proof* that Kruger's involved. I mean, who's going to believe that sleaze? Pull!"

Another clay pigeon soared. Joe blasted it and went right on talking. "All we know is that he said there was going to be another shipment on Friday."

"The whole racket better be stopped soon. Dad said they cost the real cardholders more than two million bucks so far," Frank added. "They're pretty smart—buying stuff with the fake cards, and then selling it at half price. They only use the duplicates for a couple of days, so there's almost no chance of them being caught. We've got to stop it at this end—before the cards get to the U.S."

Joe yelled "Pull!" again, but this time Frank was ready and hit the clay pigeon.

"And that means checking Kruger out, even if there's no hard evidence against him. So it looks like we're stuck sitting outside his walls, taking pictures," Joe said.

"Speaking of pictures," Frank said, "is that Alicia coming out of the darkroom with the latest batch?"

Always willing to look at Montague's dark-haired daughter, Joe turned toward the sliding glass doors in the white bungalow behind them.

No one was there.

Frank took advantage of his distraction to yell, "Pull!"

Joe whipped around, but his shot missed. Now it was his turn to glare at his brother.

Frank smiled, saying, "Now we're even." He signaled Montague that they were through.

Montague walked toward them from the trap house, carrying a manila envelope. Tall and slender, he looked fifteen years younger than his almost-seventy years. The only sign of age was his soft voice which sounded worn down after years of relentless interrogations of British villains. "Alicia left these pictures for you before she went to town," he said, handing them to Joe. "I thought you'd like to see them before you go."

The shots were all too familiar to Joe—trees, the top of Kruger's fence, his villa with the beach below. "Low tide," he said, fishing one picture out. "High tide," he added in a singsong. He fished out another. "And the big cheese himself." Joe held up a picture of Kruger. "This guy *looks* mean."

Joe's telephoto lens had caught Kruger's square face head-on. A pair of steel gray bushy eyebrows pushed their way up onto the man's forehead over a pair of calculating eyes. Kruger looked like a man who'd just been struck by a wonderfully sinister idea. He was smiling slightly, deep creases showing up in his leathery tanned face. Kruger wore a turtleneck with a sport jacket over it.

Montague grunted as he looked at the picture. "Hasn't changed much since he was captured back in forty-three. Still looks like a U-boat captain."

He slid out a photo from under the pile in Joe's hand. "I had Alicia make a copy of this from an old file." It was another picture of Kruger, showing a much younger man. His hair was dark instead of gray, and his face was lean. But his cold blue eyes looked just as evil.

"We'd just caught his sub sneaking into a quiet cove here in Bermuda," Montague explained. "I never knew what made him decide to settle here after the war."

"The climate's better than Hamburg's," Frank said.

"Maybe the *legal* climate," Montague said. "The local chaps say your man always made frequent trips to Miami and New York. I suspect Kruger's had his fingers in lots of pies."

"Better get moving," Joe said. "Who knows? Maybe we'll get lucky today."

Montague tossed them a set of car keys. "Take the old bus, but be careful—those Yank tourists are always driving on the wrong side of the road."

Laughing, the Hardys drove off, heading for Kruger's villa. The ride was beautiful along the North Shore Road to Kruger's place. After they passed the dirt road leading down to the house and the beach, they pulled the old red MG off the road into the cover of some trees. They yanked the convertible top up and locked it in place.

Hanging a pair of binoculars around his neck, Joe made his way up the rocky hill that overlooked the walled estate. "Guess I'll find my favorite rock," he said, feeling sorry for himself. He was already peering through his glasses when Frank joined him, carrying the camera with the 400mm lens.

They had a great view of the rambling, whitewashed building and the bay below them. There were no boats at the small dock, but a red-and-white buoy peacefully bobbed up and down about one hundred feet out in the calm blue-green water.

Joe was slowly scanning the house and paused at the bay window of Kruger's living room. He refocused the glasses. Then his shoulders stiffened.

"See something?" Frank asked.

"Yeah." Joe's voice was grim. "A guy— with binoculars looking at me." He turned to Frank. "We've had it for today, bro'. Should I wave bye-bye?"

"Let's just get out of here—fast!"

They tore down the rocky hill to the underbrush, where Montague's little "bus" was hidden. In minutes they were on their way back to Somerset Village.

"What do we do now?" Joe asked, rolling up his window. A stiff breeze had just come up. "If they're on to us—"

"There's nothing we can do," Frank finished for him. He pulled onto one of the many bridges that connected Bermuda's six islands. "It's so peaceful here," he said, looking at the water shimmering all around him. There were no guard rails to block his view.

Near the end of the bridge a powerful black BMW started to pass them on the right. Dark-tinted windows on the sleek performance car made it impossible to see if the driver was male or female—or if there were any passengers.

The BMW held its position, creeping toward the MG. "Why doesn't this idiot pass?" Joe grumbled.

"He's not passing!" Frank shouted suddenly. "He's trying to drive us off—"

Before Frank could hit the brakes, four thousand pounds of BMW slammed into the side of the little MG.

"Watch out!" Joe shouted.

Frank fought to stay on the bridge, but it was a lost battle. The little car spun out of control, jumping over the small curb. It rammed into the rocky slope on the left that the bridge had led up to.

The brothers were tossed forward as the car plummeted backward down the steep incline. Finally they splash-landed in thirty feet of water! As they drifted down into the crystal clear depths, Frank shook his head. Sunk, he thought. We're really and truly sunk.

Chapter

2

"I CAN'T GET the door open!" Joe rammed a forearm against the metal.

"Don't touch the door or windows!" Frank's voice was firm, but calm. Water was coming under the doors and floorboards.

Joe shook his head, groaning. "I think I must have bumped my head." He still looked a bit dazed as he took a deep breath, trying to relax himself. He hung on tightly as the little MG sank toward the soft ocean bottom and finally settled, in slow motion, onto the driver's side. Frank was moving quickly now, unbuckling both seat belts and checking out the position of the car.

"There's too much pressure from the water on your door," Frank said rapidly. "Breathe deeply and stay cool. You have to open your window just a crack."

It was hard for Joe to remain calm as he turned the car into a perfect watery grave. But he knew he had to do it. Because of the way the car had settled into the mud, Joe's window was facing toward the surface.

The water streamed in, and in less than a minute the two brothers were submerged up to their shoulders. They both pressed their faces into the narrowing air pocket above them.

"Okay," Frank said. "Take a deep breath— now open your door and then just swim toward the surface."

"Can't," Joe said, leaning into the door. "The frame's bent."

"Then open the window. Easy—don't panic. I'll be right behi—"

Frank's last words were drowned out by the water which had now filled the entire MG. Joe started cranking the handle. Slowly the window started to open more. One inch, two inches, three— His cranking came to a stop. The window was jammed!

Frank knew immediately that something had gone wrong. He leaned over his brother and began pushing down on the window. Joe continued to press against the handle. Finally the window gave way.

Joe squeezed through the tiny opening diagonally. Frank started to follow, hunching his shoulders as they scraped against the twisted frame. But a sharp piece of metal snagged a shoulder seam of his shirt. He was caught—his shoulders jammed against the two sides of the window and his arms pinned at his sides.

With his knees slightly bent, Frank planted his feet against the door on the other side of the car. Then he straightened his legs and inched his body forward. His shirt sleeve ripped as he continued forcing his way through the opening. He knew he could make it, but would he make it in time? He was almost out of oxygen.

Joe was already halfway to the surface, his head throbbing and his heart beating rapidly. He glanced behind him, expecting to see Frank swim up to him.

He instantly reversed direction when he did see Frank. Joe reached the MG in two seconds and forced his hands under Frank's arms. Then, bracing himself against the side of the car, he pushed off with his legs.

Frank was free! His face was a frightening deep red. As he kicked feebly, he prayed his natural buoyancy would carry him to the surface.

Joe pushed off against the car and made like a torpedo for the surface. He, too, was out of air.

"Uaahhhh!" The sound of the two brothers gasping for air seemed unnaturally loud after the deadly underwater silence. They bobbed up and down in the water as they gulped in great lungfuls of air.

They were only a short distance from the embankment and slowly dog-paddled to it. They pulled themselves up onto the rocky slope and collapsed onto their backs.

Their chests were still heaving when Joe spoke. "That was a close one." He coughed, then grinned. "Good thing that car didn't have electric windows!"

Frank finally smiled. "You're all right?"

"Yeah. You okay?"

"Uh-huh—but this was my favorite shirt." Frank looked at the shredded left sleeve, then grinned at Joe.

"Well, now it can be your favorite *short*-sleeved shirt," Joe offered, and the two brothers laughed.

"Whooaahh," Joe groaned as he tried to stand up, but only toppled back onto the rocks. "I guess I'm a little dizzy from punching the windshield of the car with my head. I wonder how many of my brilliant little gray cells died from the battering and the lack of oxygen?"

"I'd worry more about the damage your head did to the window," Frank said.

"My only worry right now is getting home

13

and getting dry.'' The bump on the head had done nothing to affect Joe's impatience.

"What's your hurry?" Frank asked. "It's a long climb up and then a long walk back to the village. I think we should just take it easy for a few minutes.''

Frank glanced up to the road to see if anyone was observing them. Joe lay back with his eyes closed, still taking long, deep breaths and occasionally rubbing the spot on his forehead, which was working its way into a lump. Frank broke the long silence.

"No one around. Nobody would have even known we went off the bridge.''

"Except whoever was in the BMW," Joe reminded him.

"Did you get a look at anyone?" Frank asked.

"Couldn't see a thing through those windows, and he, she, or it was already alongside us by the time I looked. I don't even know if the car followed us from Kruger's. But somebody tried to kill us, and that means we *are* getting close to something.'' Joe frowned.

After the brothers had rested, they climbed up over the rocks to the road.

"We can either walk back to those stores we passed and phone Montague, or try to hitch," Frank said.

Joe stuck out his thumb and started walking

backward toward Somerset. "I don't think I want to tell Montague on the phone that the car he's loved since 1968 is thirty feet underwater."

"But I don't know who's going to pick us up looking like this," said Frank. "We look so disheveled."

" 'Disheveled'?" Joe repeated. "I think you were underwater too long—you sound like Aunt Gertrude!"

As Joe stretched out his thumb again, a pickup truck bounced by and came to a wobbly stop.

"Need a lift?" the long-faced, unshaven man behind the wheel shouted.

The brothers ran toward the truck and started to jump in the back.

"You can ride up front," the driver insisted. "A little water isn't going to hurt this baby. What happened to you guys?"

"You know how it goes," Joe answered, hoping his vague reply would do.

The lean man nodded his head and grinned. He dropped the brothers at the driveway that led up to Montague's villa.

As they were closing the door to the house, Montague called down from upstairs. "That you, boys?"

Joe cleared his throat, which suddenly had become dry. "Uh, yes, we're back."

"I didn't hear the car pull up. I'll be right down."

Frank and Joe looked at each other in awkward silence. They had no idea how to tell Montague what happened to his "bus." But their host made it easy for them—the moment he walked downstairs he knew something was wrong. He cut off Frank's explanation about the MG. "Never mind the car—are you boys okay?"

"We're fine," the boys assured him, relieved that Montague was more concerned about them than his car. They told him about the attempted killing.

"You'll have to report this to the Hamilton police," Montague told them. "*And* you'll need some way to get around. There are no rental cars on the island, but you can rent mopeds. There's a place in Hamilton. Let's see . . ." He looked at his watch. "Alicia said she'd be back at four—that'll give you time for a wash-up and rest.

"Alicia and I have a five o'clock engagement we can't break, but we can drop you at the ferry to Hamilton."

Later they heard a car pull into the driveway, and in a minute Montague's eighteen-year-old daughter burst in. Her sparkling dark brown eyes widened in concern as she listened to a recap of the boys' story. It left her pale under her smooth tan. Her short black hair danced as she turned from Frank to Joe, her eyes drawn to the bump on Joe's head. "You're hurt!"

"Not enough to slow me down," Joe told her. "We'd better hurry, so we can make the bike rental place before closing."

The quiet of the ferry ride to Hamilton was shattered by the sound of the ferry crunching against the dock. After the brothers left the boat, they walked the three blocks to the moped rental place.

The bikes were all the same—squat-looking scooters with small, fat wheels—so the choice was easy. Frank handed the burly attendant his father's credit card, which had been given to him for emergencies.

"I'm sorry," the salesman said after making a phone call. "I cannot allow you to have the bikes. Your credit card is more than three thousand dollars over the limit, and I've been instructed to cut up your card."

"We haven't spent anywhere near that much!" Frank stared at the man.

"You can't destroy our card," Joe said, leaning into the counter as if he'd push his way right through it. "And you've got to give us those bikes."

"Sorry, chum," the attendant repeated in

his flawless British accent. "You must take it up with the credit card company."

"The card!" Joe demanded, his hand stretched out.

"Take it easy," Frank cautioned. "It's not his fault."

"Yeah, well it's not *our* fault, either, and why should—"

"Come on, Joe," Frank said, interrupting him and grabbing him by the arm. "We'll straighten this out later. It's getting late and we still have to see the police."

Frank and Joe walked through the narrow two-lane streets and watched as the shops were beginning to close. When they were two blocks from the station, they heard the sound of a car behind them picking up speed. A maroon sedan shot past them, then screeched to a halt, its red brake lights flashing on. Then, the two clear backup lights came on as the car roared back to them.

Two large, well-dressed men jumped out of the car and approached them. One of them, a tall black man wearing a conservative pin-striped suit, pulled back his coat to reveal a gun tucked into his belt. The other man, shorter, opened his dark blue suit and drew a small revolver from a shoulder holster.

"Just hold it right there," he said. "Don't do anything stupid."

The blue suit stood in front of the Hardys as the tall man with the hat walked behind them. Joe, standing in front of Frank, could hear the click-clack as the tall man snapped handcuffs on Frank's bare wrists. Two more clicks and Joe, too, was handcuffed. Finally the tall man spoke:

"You're under arrest for fraud, conspiracy to defraud, and credit card counterfeiting."

Chapter

3

"COUNTERFEITING! WHAT'RE YOU talking about?" Joe turned his head back and forth between the two men.

"Who are you?" Frank asked.

Blue suit holstered his gun with one hand as he reached into his back pocket with the other. "I'm Bill Baylis," he said as he produced identification. "And this is Walt Conway. I'm from the Interagency Banking Commission, and Detective Conway is with the Bermuda police, assigned to work with me."

"We happened to see you leaving Bernhard Kruger's," the man called Conway chimed in. "And we know about the faked credit card you just tried to use."

"There must be some mistake," Frank insisted.

"Where've we heard *that* one before?" countered Baylis. "Let's go to police headquarters. You can tell your story there."

"We were just on our way there," Joe admitted, realizing how phony it sounded.

"We're private investigators," Frank told them, "staying with Alfred Montague."

"Into the car." The tall man's tone made it clear he wasn't interested in any more conversation. He opened the back door and ushered them in.

Within minutes they were seated in the office of Chief Boulton. The blond police chief with his dark walrus mustache was bigger than Biff Hooper and very impressive in his immaculate, all-white uniform. He seemed out of place in an office where every flat surface was cluttered with papers, books, and boxes. He looked at the boys with cold blue eyes. "May I see some identification, please?"

"We do get one phone call, don't we?" Joe asked, half-joking.

"Of course," the chief responded. "Local or long distance?"

"Local. We're staying with Alfred Montague. He's a retired policeman—do you know him?" The chief nodded. "He'll vouch for us." Joe dialed Montague's number. After the seventh ring, he hung up, remembering Montague's five o'clock appointment.

Frank explained to the three men the purpose of their visit to Bermuda and why they had the Kruger villa under surveillance. He told them about Fenton Hardy's involvement in the case back in the U.S. and how ironic it was that they were now being held for a crime they were trying to stop.

"I know of your father," the chief said, lightening up a little. "Shall I ring him?"

The boys hated to use their dad to bail them out, but after exchanging a brief look, they nodded their agreement.

Chief Boulton called Fenton Hardy, spoke briefly with him, and turned the phone over to Frank. Frank filled his father in on everything that had happened so far. He learned that his father hadn't put more than two hundred dollars on the credit card that the merchant confiscated.

The chief got back on the phone. "Makes sense to me," he said after listening silently for a long time. "Fine, then. I'll call Chief Collig in Bayport. Then if everything checks out, I'll be happy to release your boys and give them all the help I can." After a quick goodbye, the chief hung up.

Frank asked why they had been arrested when they hadn't done anything but try to use a card over its limit. And Chief Boulton confessed that they thought Frank and Joe might be couriers for the counterfeit credit card gang because they had been seen leaving Kruger's earlier. And then, when they tried to use the overdrawn card, they had decided to bring the Hardys in with the hope of sweating information out of them about Kruger.

Before they were released, Frank and Joe officially reported the incident with the black BMW. Although they couldn't connect the attempt on their lives with their investigation of Kruger, there didn't seem to be any other explanation.

Chief Boulton gave Frank and Joe some additional information about the counterfeiting racket. The police thought that stolen blank cards were being shipped to Bermuda—possibly from Puerto Rico. They were "punched" in Bermuda and then sent to the U.S. for distribution. The police suspected Kruger, but they didn't have enough evidence to search the man's house.

"That's it," the chief said. "That's everything I have on Kruger. I can't get your credit card back, but if you're going to continue your investigation, I'll call the moped agency and arrange for you to rent two bikes. Meanwhile, your father said he would arrange to get you a different card."

"Thanks," the brothers replied.

"And if you're short of cash in the meantime, just let me know."

Frank and Joe smiled, pleased that the chief had turned out to be so good-natured.

"Now just fill out these accident report forms," the chief continued. "And list everything that was in the car when it sank."

"Oh no!" Joe blurted out. "I completely forgot about the stuff in the trunk." Joe's face fell as he realized out loud that both cameras were thirty feet underwater.

"And the binoculars," Frank added.

"You can rent scuba gear across the street," the chief suggested, "if you're in the mood for a do-it-yourself rescue. But I don't know how good the cameras will be after *that* dunking!"

"One of them was an underwater camera," Joe explained. "We used it when we went diving near Kruger's dock a couple days ago."

"I'll ring the scuba shop and make the arrangements."

It was almost six-thirty by the time Frank and Joe loaded rented scuba gear on the back of the mopeds to ride out to the MG. It was a pleasant ride. The summer light made the pastel ice-cream colors of the houses outside Hamilton shimmer. The temperature was still warm, even though an ocean breeze blew across the narrow highway.

"Here's the spot," shouted Frank, pointing down to where he knew the little car lay. Joe pulled up next to Frank, parking beside a pile of rocks.

"Do you want to set up on the flat rock down there?" Joe asked, extending his arm toward a flat rock below them.

"Looks good." Frank nodded.

In fifteen minutes the boys were ready. Joe had stuck a spare key to the trunk into a small pouch attached to his weight belt.

"The water's so still," Frank said.

"Yeah. It's hard to believe it almost buried us."

Frank and Joe slipped into the warm water and dived. It didn't take long to spot the MG, which had sunk another two feet into the soft sand. Joe motioned to Frank to check the inside of the car for the binoculars while he swam around to the trunk.

Frank was able to force the passenger door open very slowly, granting him easy access to the car's interior. He found the binoculars and was looking to see if anything else had been left inside when he heard a sharp bang against the metal frame of the car. He turned to see Joe waving his arm for Frank to come.

Joe's eyes were opened wide under the small

mask, and Frank knew instantly something was wrong. He swam to Joe at the rear of the MG.

The trunk lid was wide open and bent out of shape. Frank saw that the lid hadn't gotten twisted from the accident. Someone had forced it open. The two cameras were gone!

Joe could understand why they had been run off the road—if Kruger was behind it. But why would he order someone to dive thirty feet underwater to take two cameras from the submerged car? Was he afraid of what the film might show? But would the film even be all right after getting wet?

As Joe's mind was wandering, searching for answers, Frank was swimming around the MG, looking for clues. Trying to get his younger brother's attention, Frank clanged the base of his knife against Joe's tank, snapping him out of his daydream. Joe nodded after Frank made a swirling motion with his hand indicating they should scour the area.

The water was so clear that there was enough light to see even at thirty feet, although Frank was using a flashlight anyway.

They finished their underwater search, and Frank gave Joe a thumbs-up sign. It was time to surface. The two brothers swam toward the darkening sunlight above and climbed out near the rocks where they had left their gear.

"That was a waste of time," Joe said, pulling off his face mask.

Frank shook his head, disagreeing. "I don't think so. We learned that Kruger's really afraid that we might have something on him."

"That's what I figured. A picture of something," Joe said.

"Could be. Or maybe he just wanted our stuff to see if they could learn more about us. What else *was* in the trunk? Do you remember?" Frank asked.

"Let's see," Joe replied, closing his eyes and trying to visualize the trunk. "My bag, which had a change of clothes and our towels and swim trunks, and some shells— maybe . . ."

"What about that lifesaver we found on the beach near Kruger's villa?" Frank was talking about a ring-shaped life preserver that must have fallen from a boat and been washed ashore.

"That's right." Joe nodded, then stared at his brother. "But what would anyone want that for?"

"Nothing—unless it belonged to them in the first place!"

Frank and Joe gathered up their gear for the trek back up to the mopeds. They checked the ground carefully for any signs left by the underwater thieves during their approach or get-away.

"Someone might have walked over here, but that doesn't tell us anything," Joe mused, talking to himself.

"I don't see anything," Frank said.

When they reached the bikes, they checked for tire tracks or footprints—anything that might help them later in establishing the thieves' identity.

After Joe loaded his gear onto the moped, he scanned the surroundings. "They had to leave something behind," he said. "No one's that good."

"Looks like they were careful. Pros always are."

"But maybe not careful enough!" Joe had just noticed something glinting under a low bush.

Frank followed Joe's gaze about fifteen feet from where they had climbed down to the water. A small object was shining, reflecting the early-evening light. "I see it!"

"I hope it's not just a pack of cigarettes or something," Joe said as he jogged over to the bush. "Whoa—this just might be our first clue. Looks like a credit card!" Joe smiled.

"Well?" Frank said.

"Well," Joe mimicked, "it *is* a credit card, a Bank Eurocard." The sun was gleaming off the card's hologram. As Joe looked closer, his triumphant grin disappeared.

"Well?" Frank urged.

"It'll be very easy to track down the person who owns this," Joe continued. "According to the name on the card, it belongs to—Alfred Montague!"

Chapter
4

"MONTAGUE?" FRANK REPEATED, complete disbelief on his face.

"Alfred Montague. That's what it says. I can't believe he's involved in this."

Frank agreed. "Me, neither. There must be *some* explanation."

"If there isn't?"

"If there isn't"—Frank paused—"we might be staying in the home of someone who's trying to kill us!"

"What do we do? How do we find out?"

Frank thought for a second. "We'll ask him." He made it sound as if it would be the easiest thing in the world. But Frank knew the confrontation with Montague would be awkward—and possibly dangerous.

"Okay. But I'd feel a lot better if Alicia wasn't around when we meet with Montague." He looked at his watch. "Almost eight o'clock. They should be home by now. Why don't I give her a call—think of something to get her out of the house," Joe suggested.

Frank nodded and got on his moped to join his brother. After a few minutes of riding, Frank pointed out a pay phone next to a small roadside restaurant. Joe dropped two coins into the box, then slowly dialed. He was still trying to think of some reason to get Alicia away from the house.

"Hello? Alicia? . . . Hi . . ." Joe was thinking in double time. Maybe he could ask her to meet him somewhere, then he and Frank could go to the house when she left. But he rejected that idea because it would leave her stranded. "Do you, uh, feel like coming out to meet me?" he asked, still fumbling for words. ". . . Oh . . . Where? . . . Could you give that to me again? . . . Wait, let me write it down." Joe fished for a pencil and then jotted something down as Alicia talked. "Thanks," he concluded. "I—we'll see you soon."

Thoughtfully Joe replaced the phone on its hook and walked back to where Frank was waiting, straddling his moped.

"Could you get her out of the house?" Frank asked.

31

"She can't go anyplace because Montague had to borrow her car. But she did say she got a strange call about half an hour ago from some guy she didn't know. He said that Montague was supposed to be meeting with him, but he hadn't shown. And this guy"—he paused to check his notes—"Martin Powers, said the meeting was urgent. He left her his address."

"Well, where is he? Let's go check it out." Frank was ready to take off.

Joe checked his notes again. "Saint George's Harbor." He handed the note to Frank on which he had hastily scrawled "Martin Powers, #1 Blue Vista."

The two scooters lurched forward as Frank and Joe sped off toward St. George.

It was dark when the Hardys drove down into town. They parked their bikes and carried their scuba gear into a small café.

"Yes, I do know where that is," said the proprietor after looking at the address. "You can leave your gear in the back room and then I'll accompany you outside and set you in the right direction."

Joe and Frank found a clear corner for their stuff, then followed the proprietor outside.

"Just go through the square there," the man explained as he pointed, "and take a right out onto the quay. It should be one of the boats out on the left of the dock.''

''Boats?'' both brothers said simultaneously. Joe stared at the man. ''You mean this address is a boat?''

''Definitely! *One Blue Vista* is the name of a boat. Happy sailing!''

Sailing wasn't what they were thinking of when Frank and Joe located the boat that had the name painted in bright blue letters across its stern. Martin Powers's boat took up an entire corner of the dock. ''That's no sloop,'' Joe remarked. ''That's a full-size yacht.''

''I wonder where this Powers guy is. Doesn't look like anybody's on board.'' Frank's observation was pretty obvious—there wasn't a light on.

''You want to have a look?'' Joe asked.

''It's trespassing,'' Frank reminded his younger brother.

''Yeah, but we're trying to find out what happened to Montague. Maybe he's on board—hurt or something. We should check it out.''

Joe took out his small underwater flashlight. He was going on board, with or without Frank.

''Okay,'' Frank finally agreed. ''But let's make it quick—someone may come soon, and there's no back door to *this* house.'' He followed Joe onto the deck of the large boat, walking silently in case someone really was on board. The sound of the water lapping against the side of the boat drowned out the creaking of the deck under the boys' weight.

"Here's the door that leads down to the cabins," Frank whispered.

Joe's flashlight lit up the small latch on the cabin-house door. Frank pulled on it, and the small door swung open.

"I'll go first," Joe said. Frank checked to make sure no one from shore could see what they were doing. The dock was empty. "Follow me," Joe said, forcing Frank's attention back.

The two brothers moved stealthily down the few steps into the small living compartment. "Watch yourself," said Frank from behind.

Just as Frank spoke Joe tripped over something, stumbling noisily forward. The flashlight flew from his hand, to make a hard landing against the wooden floor.

Frank winced as he heard the sound of breaking glass, followed by the lopping sound of the flashlight as it rolled across the floor. The light winked on and off with each turn of the flashlight. "You okay?"

Joe had landed on one knee, but recovered quickly. "Yeah. The lens on the flashlight broke, but the light still works." Joe reached down and picked it up, shaking it gently every time the small light flickered out.

"Are you clumsy, or what?" Frank asked his brother.

"I tripped over something," Joe said, annoyed.

Joe shone the light on the steps that had led down into the cabin. "But there's nothing on the stairs." Just then the light reflected off a thin wire that ran across the last step.

"Uh-oh," said Frank. "I don't think that's a regulation part of the boat."

Frank took the light from Joe and followed the wire with it. The dim glow barely illuminated the corner of the cabin, where the wire eventually led to a small box about fifteen inches square.

Frank's worst fears were realized. He now could hear the faint ticking of a clock. "Is that what I think it is?" Joe asked, knowing what Frank's answer would be.

"Yep. It's a bomb," Frank said, moving quickly to examine it more closely. "You triggered it when you tripped on that wire."

"Then why didn't it go off?" Joe asked.

Frank was shining the light on two wires that ran from the little box to a small digital clock set in its face. "It's a time delay." Frank stared at the changing numbers on the clock. "And we have less than six seconds! Hit the deck! It's going to blow!''

Joe dived into the darkness, overturning a small table, which he scrambled behind.

Frank had gingerly picked up the bomb when he shouted for Joe to take cover. He had had to drop the flashlight, and the room was now in total blackness. For only a fraction of a second Frank stood motionless. Then he noticed the light coming in from the outside through a small porthole. Four seconds left.

Praying that the porthole was open, Frank rushed toward it.

Two seconds.

"Here goes!" He pitched the small box toward the light. But just before the bomb reached the small, circular opening, Frank saw a reflection on the glass, and he knew the tiny porthole was closed!

One second later the room filled with a flash of hot, bright whiteness as the bomb exploded—inside the small cabin!

Chapter
5

THE ROAR OF the explosion was deafening. Within seconds an entire side of *One Blue Vista* was blown out and engulfed in flames.

"Frank! Frank!" Joe cried out, pulling himself free of debris.

There was no reply.

Joe tried to push down his thoughts of losing Frank. He had been protected, in the far corner behind the collapsed table. But Frank had been in the middle of the room, completely exposed.

Fire was spreading rapidly through the tiny cabin. Furniture, books, and papers had been thrown around the room by the force of the blast. Shattered glass covered the deck, and heavy black smoke fell from the ceiling. Joe saw their plastic flashlight melted into the floor.

Only a moment earlier Joe had been in desperate need of light. Now the glow from the flames was blinding.

"Frank! Where are you?" Joe knew his brother would answer if he could.

Then Joe saw him. Frank's legs were sticking out from under a door just a few feet away. Obviously he had tried to protect himself by crouching between the bulkhead and a closet door, which he'd pulled open just before the blast. The door must have been blown from its hinges, and now lay on top of Frank's lifeless body.

"I'll get you out!" Joe yelled as he moved on all fours through the rubble toward his brother. Frank continued to lie motionless. Smoke was beginning to fill the room from the ceiling down. Joe tore the door off his brother, then he grabbed Frank under his arms and crawled through the smoke, dragging him.

"We'll make it," he said, not even knowing if Frank was dead or alive. "Here we go." He stood up and threw Frank over his shoulder and charged up what remained of the steps.

Aware that when the fire reached the fuel tanks for the engines there would be another explosion, Joe darted to the guard rail. He shifted Frank so he lay across his shoulders, clambered over the rail, and plunged into the oily waters.

"Got to swim clear," he kept saying. Side-stroking with one arm around Frank's chest, Joe swam parallel to the main dock toward the next pier. Joe suddenly realized he was getting some help. Frank was moving his legs and kicking feebly! "That's it!" Joe cried, as they moved a little faster. "Swim, swim!"

The wailing of the fire engine and ambulance sirens cut through the crackle of the flames. Then all sound was drowned out by a tremendous roar. The fire had reached the boat's fuel tanks.

"Down!" Joe yelled, pulling his brother underwater with him. They felt the force of the new explosion ripple through the cushioning effect of the water, but they were safe. They had swum far enough away from the yacht.

When they came up for air, Joe checked Frank out to see how badly he was hurt. He could see numerous cuts and bruises on his brother's arms, but Frank's face was okay except for a large bump over his left eye. "Are you all right?"

Frank groaned. "What happened?"

"You were on an exploding boat," Joe reminded him.

"Ohhh," Frank groaned, stretching his arms and neck. "I forget, does that make us flotsam or jetsam?"

Joe smiled. "How do you feel?"

"Like a soccer ball—after a game. Are you okay?"

"I think so, but I've been too busy saving you to check!"

Exhausted, the brothers were slowly dog-paddling toward a pier when suddenly they were bathed in a circle of bright light. It was coming from a spotlight bobbing up and down in the water. It had to be a boat, the boys knew, even though they couldn't see a thing beyond the blinding glare. The source of the light reached them in a few seconds, and the two Hardys could hear excited voices over the roar of the boat's engines.

"Grab my hand!" a voice ordered as the boat pulled beside them. "Come on, son, I've got you," said one man as he grabbed Frank and pulled him up over the side of the boat. "You next, friend," another man said.

"Easy does it!" the first voice said. "You boys all right?" And before anybody could answer, he added, "Just lie there and take it easy."

Both Joe and Frank could tell from the crew's brisk, precise movements that they'd gone through this drill often. The uniforms on the crew members and the blinking blue and red light on the stern told the Hardys they were aboard a police boat. Joe spoke first. "So what happened after I took cover?"

"I tossed the bomb and then realized that the porthole was closed," said Frank. "The bomb must have exploded just before it hit the porthole—it blew the glass right out and then released its full force outside the boat."

"Yeah," Joe agreed, "that must be why the room wasn't trashed more than it was." He shook his head. "Good timing. A few seconds sooner and the bomb would have bounced off that glass right back at you. A few seconds later would have been *too* late."

"I took a dive for the corner just after I threw the bomb," Frank explained. "I didn't have time to get into the closet, but I was able to yank the door open. And then the lights went out."

The two had almost forgotten they were surrounded by a small group of police and Coast Guard. One of them leaned over to question the brothers. His eyes narrowed and he stared directly at Frank. "Now, why were you trying to plant a bomb on Martin Powers's boat?"

"Are you kidding?" Joe said, exasperated. "We were trying to get the bomb *off* the boat."

"How did you know there was a bomb *on* the boat?" the harbor policeman continued.

"I tripped over it," Joe confessed, before he realized how silly it sounded.

"Just what were you doing on the boat?"

But before Joe could answer, the police boat

had reached the pier and the two brothers were helped onto the dock, where a few curious onlookers had gathered. Six or seven people stood around immediately in front of them, one taking pictures. Someone shouted from the back of the small group, "Arrest these two! Arrest them! They blew up my partner's boat! They've killed him!"

"Oh, no," Frank said. "Here we go again." He could see the man's fist waving above the heads of the others.

"Arrest them," the stranger kept insisting.

"No need to worry, we've got them now, and we'll take care of them," one of the officers said as he handcuffed the two brothers.

"Hold it," Joe objected, turning his head away from the blinding flashes of the photographer's camera. "We didn't *do* anything." But no one listened.

Then the stranger, a squat man with bushy, steel-gray eyebrows, emerged from the back of the small crowd. "Lock them up!" he yelled, staring at the two of them as he moved closer.

Joe immediately recognized the well-dressed, gray-haired man from the photos he had been looking at earlier that same day. "Kruger!" he shouted.

The sinister-looking German curled the corner of his lip into an evil smile. "Yes, Kruger—Bernhard Kruger." He let out a short laugh, and then turned and walked toward the burning boat.

"*He's* the one that should be arrested!" Joe yelled, pointing into the crowd. But no one was listening as he and Frank were being towed toward the waiting police car. Joe was furious. "Wait a minute!" he objected, struggling to turn around. But as he looked back, he saw that Kruger had disappeared into the curious crowd.

Joe and Frank were quickly checked by one of the medics who had arrived and then were escorted into the waiting patrol car. As they were pulling away, they turned and could still see the glow from the fire. Fifteen minutes after their ordeal the two Hardys were sitting in the St. George police station, wrapped in blankets and drinking hot tea.

Joe and Frank sipped their tea and explained to the officers who they were, what they were doing on the boat, and what their connection was with Kruger.

Within a few minutes a heavyset, dark-skinned man with short, curly hair that looked as if it had been flecked with white entered the small interrogation room. "I'm Captain Hodges," he said to the Hardys. He listened to the boys' story from his chief officer, then immediately called Chief Boulton.

"George Hodges here," the brothers heard

him say. "Sorry to ring so late, but we had a little fire here on the docks. I have a couple of kids with me who claim to be friends of yours."

Joe put his face in his hands as he listened to Chief Hodges explain the situation to Chief Boulton in Hamilton. "Great!" he mumbled. "We managed to get arrested not once, but *twice* in less than a week."

"We haven't arrested you—yet," Captain Hodges said as he hung up the phone. This time he finished his comment with a broad smile. "You're just here for questioning. It *seems* your story checks out. Your identification looks legitimate. I suggest you lay these out overnight on some paper toweling," he said as he returned the Hardys' ID cards. "And I think once you fill out some papers and sign a statement, we can let you go."

"You mean we're being released?" Frank asked, still somewhat dazed.

"Yes," Hodges assured them. "But remember that even the famous Hardy brothers can be arrested for trespassing and illegal entry."

The brothers nodded, aware that he could have detained them if he wanted.

"Chief Boulton asked me to tell you to watch out for yourselves," Hodges said with a smile. Joe grinned and shifted in his seat.

"But," he said softly, his tone turning more

serious, "I also have some bad news. Walt Conway, a detective from our force, wasn't so lucky. He was shot this afternoon and is in critical condition."

"Shot?" both brothers chorused.

"He was ambushed a couple of hours ago as he was getting out of his car in front of his home."

"Did they catch the guy?" Joe asked.

"All we know is that there were probably two men. An eyewitness said the shooter's car pulled away at just about the same time the shot was fired, so we assume one person drove while another handled the gun." His chest heaved as he took a long breath. "The doctors removed one slug from him—a twenty-two."

Hodges paused a second to reflect on the outbreak of violence on his usually peaceful island. "These incidents are starting to get out of hand. And if they are all related as you say—" He paused again, shaking his head in frustration. "If only we could get something on this Kruger fellow."

It was almost midnight when the boys drove up to the Montague house on their mopeds. Alicia was up, waiting at the screen door. She was standing rigid, pale and distraught. "Are you all right? I heard what happened on the news. When I called the Saint George police, they said you had already left. I thought Dad might be with you. Was he in the explosion?''

"Whoa," Frank said, interrupting her. The boys were still standing outside. "Slow down. May we come in?''

Alicia didn't realize that she was blocking the doorway. "I'm sorry. Come in, sit down.'' Although normally in control, Alicia was terribly excited and tense now. "I'm so worried,'' she confessed. "Did you see Dad? He hasn't come home. And he was supposed to have been at that boat that blew up. I'm terrified something's happened to him!''

"We didn't see him. But I'm sure he's fine.'' Joe tried to sound very confident. "He wasn't on the boat—I'm positive.'' He was worried about Alicia's father, and almost forgot that Montague might have been the one who tried to have them killed!

"Let's change our clothes," Frank suggested, still damp from their evening plunge. "And then we'll go out and see if we can find him.'' But he knew that with nothing to go on, their search would probably be fruitless.

"Did you call the police?" Joe asked.

"I mentioned it when I spoke with the Saint George police, but they didn't know anything. And if the Hamilton police knew something happened to Dad, they'd call me.'' Alicia sounded much calmer now.

"Shh!" Joe said, interrupting her. "I heard a noise outside."

The three listened in silence.

"Sounds like we have visitors," Frank said. "Maybe our friend from the boat wants a second chance."

Joe reacted quickly. "I'll go out the back and circle around."

"Go upstairs," Frank whispered to Alicia.

"But what's going on?"

"I'll explain later." He moved quietly toward the front door.

Alicia backed up the stairs as Frank positioned himself behind the front door. He could hear someone approaching the house very slowly.

Joe peered out from around the side of the house. He moved forward silently and crouched behind a low bush on the side of the driveway as he watched someone crawl along toward the front door. The person, on all fours, was moving stealthily across the front lawn.

Joe stole out from behind the bush, then sneaked around behind the prowler and moved up on him without a sound. With the accuracy of a mountain cat, he lunged forward, knocking the man flat.

"Got you!"

Frank burst through the front door, ready to help.

But the man trapped under Joe wasn't putting up a fight at all. He just lay there, motionless. Joe had lifted himself off the limp body and was flipping the man onto his back as Alicia thrust her head out an upstairs window.

She screamed. Frank looked up at her silhouette in the window, then turned back to Joe when he heard his brother gasp. Joe's prisoner was Alfred Montague!

Chapter

6

"MONTAGUE! CAN YOU hear me?" Joe asked the semiconscious man.

Frank turned to see if Alicia was still at the upstairs window. But she was already at the front door, running toward them.

"Oh, no!" Alicia exclaimed as she saw the limp body of her father. "He's bleeding!"

Blood trickled down the side of Montague's face from a cut just above his left eye; his eye was swollen and turning black and blue. His chin was cut but had stopped bleeding. Montague's eyelids began to flutter open.

"He's coming to," Joe reported.

"Let's get him into the house." Frank took Montague by the legs while Joe carefully lifted the wounded man under the shoulders. Alicia wanted to help, so she ran ahead and propped open the front door, then cleared off the living-room sofa. "Put him right here."

They laid him down on the couch, propping his head up with one of the cushions. Alicia went to get some water and a washcloth. Besides the bruises on his face, he had a large lump on the back of his head, and a two-inch spot of his hair was matted down with dried blood.

Returning from the kitchen Alicia asked, "Is he all right?" There was a slight tremor in her voice.

"I don't think there are any broken bones," Joe announced, "and hopefully no internal injuries."

Montague lay still, moving only his eyes. Although fully conscious, he still looked dazed and bewildered. "What happened?"

"That's what we were going to ask you," said Frank. "Boy, that must have been some fight!"

"I don't remember any fight," Montague wheezed. "I just remember being hit on the head and then waking up on the front lawn with *everything* hurting. I don't know if someone was trying to kill me or not."

"I don't think so," Joe said. "If someone had been trying to kill you, you'd have more than a bump on the head. It looks to me as if someone wanted to teach you a lesson—"

"Or make you look bad," Frank added.

"Dad—"

"I'll be all right, honey. Now, don't you worry." Montague tried to calm Alicia. His words were clear, and they all knew he hadn't been badly hurt. He then turned his attention to Frank and Joe. "What happened to you fellows?"

"Never mind us, what happened to *you?*" It had been a trying day—an endless day—a day that was making even Frank impatient to find answers.

"I went out to try to help you fellows after I heard you were kidnapped."

"Heard what?" Frank and Joe said together.

"I received a phone call when we got home from our five o'clock appointment. The voice—some man's, I didn't recognize it—said the two of you had been kidnapped and that if I didn't believe him, he would send me Frank's ring—still attached to his finger. He told me to meet them at the Gibbs Hill Lighthouse, alone."

"Then?" Frank asked.

"Well, I don't remember exactly what he said, but I just assumed it would have taken more than one person to subdue both of you. Anyway, I drove out to the lighthouse without even telling Alicia, and as I was waiting, someone cracked me on the head. That's the last thing I remember until I woke up on the front lawn.''

Frank hesitated a minute, unsure whether Montague was a victim or a mastermind. He brought out the credit card Joe had found. Frank knew the card had been found *before* Montague's abduction, but he wanted to hear his host's reaction—or excuse. "Did you lose your Bank Eurocard?" he asked, trying not to make it sound like an accusation.

"Don't know," Montague replied. "Let me check my wallet." He reached beneath him as if he were going to pull his wallet from his back pocket, but his hand returned empty. "I seem to have lost my entire wallet," he said. "I could have lost it at any time today, because I don't know when I checked it last."

Joe's mouth tightened as he listened to Montague speak. Frank could see that Joe was having difficulty believing Montague, and although Frank really liked the man, he didn't know *what* to think.

"We'd better call the police," Joe said after Montague had finished his story.

"No," Montague said. "There's nothing they can do now. And I'm too tired to handle any questions right now anyway."

Frank and Joe tried to convince Montague

to call them, but their host insisted on leaving the police out of it. "I'm going to bed now," he announced, rising suddenly from the couch. He turned and walked toward the stairway.

Alicia jumped up and went over to her father, gently taking his arm above the elbow. "See you in the morning, boys," she said, helping her father up the stairs.

"What do you think?" Joe asked his brother.

"I don't know what to think," Frank admitted. "His bruises were real, that's for sure."

"*I* think it's time to check out this house. If Montague's involved in any of this, there might be a clue."

"Maybe you're right, but I've done enough for one day." Frank could no longer hide his weariness. "And what if we're wrong? I really don't feel comfortable going through his drawers and closets. We *are* his guests, you know."

"His guests *or* his victims," Joe quickly pointed out.

"Fine," Frank muttered as he headed upstairs to the guest room. "Let me know what you uncover—in the morning."

Joe decided he would work on his own. He tiptoed around the living room, opening drawers, searching behind curtains and under seat cushions, lifting lamps, and moving books, not knowing *what* he was looking for.

Then he went into the small study off the living room and opposite the kitchen. He crossed to an easy chair with a small end table next to it and pulled open the drawer in the table. His question was answered when he saw—on top of the pens—a small revolver.

Joe reached for the gun, not concerned with protecting fingerprints since it was undoubtedly Montague's gun and his prints would be on it. He lifted the gun to his nose. It's been fired recently, he thought. The .22 revolver still had two bullets left in it. Although he and Frank hadn't dodged any bullets yet, Joe remembered that Walt Conway had been shot that afternoon with a .22.

He brought the gun upstairs, excited to show his brother, but Frank was already fast asleep. No point waking him now, Joe decided. Can't do a ballistics check until tomorrow, anyway.

Joe took off his shoes and lay down on the bed next to Frank's, thinking about everything that had taken place since early morning. He held the gun, after making certain the safety was on, and turned it over again and again. He was thinking about Kruger, the black car, the boat—and Montague—and as he lay there trying to put some of the pieces of the puzzle together, he shut his eyes and fell fast asleep.

*   *   *

"Let's go!" Frank said, what seemed like only moments later to Joe.

He moaned. "I just fell aslee—" He stopped short when he saw it was light outside.

"Let's go," Frank repeated. "Nine o'clock! You want to slip on some pajamas so we can go into town?"

Joe didn't understand his brother's joke until he realized that he had fallen asleep with his clothes on. "I feel awful," he said.

"You look it. And since when have you taken to sleeping with a gun?"

"A gun? Why would I— Oh, *that* gun." Joe saw the revolver on the bed next to him and realized he must have fallen asleep with it. "I found it last night in the end table in the study. I know it's Montague's gun, and the interesting thing is, it's been fired recently. I thought we could take it down to the police lab today."

"Good. And then I think we should head back to Kruger's."

"After being spotted yesterday?"

"Maybe they won't expect us." Frank picked up a towel that had been tossed over the arm of an easy chair and threw it at Joe. "I called the police in Hamilton and Saint George just a minute ago. Divers went out early this morning to check out the MG, and experts sifted through the rubble of *One Blue Vista*. Nobody came up with anything. So, Kruger is still our best lead." He paused and put both hands on his hips. "Now, wouldn't you like to get ready for the day's detective work?" he asked, kidding his brother.

Joe hung the towel around his neck, smiled, and headed groggily into the bathroom. "Another day, another adventure," he mumbled.

It didn't take Joe long to get ready, and he soon joined his brother and Alicia in the kitchen for a light breakfast. Alicia agreed to let them use her car, since neither she nor her father had any plans for the day.

By nine-forty-five they were on their way. They went into Hamilton first and stopped off at the police station to drop off Montague's gun. Then they drove on to Kruger's.

They pulled off the road into a small clearing behind a clump of trees, about a hundred yards in front of the place where they had parked the day before. "Let's leave the car here," Frank suggested, "and walk the rest of the way. It should make it harder for them to spot us," he added. He stopped and pointed at a small boat he noticed heading into shore. The all-white boat looked about twenty-six feet long. Frank couldn't see any crew.

"It's aimed right for Kruger's dock," Joe said. He paused and stared at the boat and dock, a puzzled look on his face. "I took a picture of that dock the other day. Something's not right." He tried to remember how everything had looked the last time they were there. "Wait a minute! Do buoys move?"

"Sure. They bob up and down all the time."

"No, I mean from one spot to another," Joe explained.

"No," Frank said. "They're anchored down, so they can be used as markers."

"Or signals!" Joe felt a rush of excitement. "When I took a picture last time, that buoy was on the other side of the dock. I'm positive. It was closer to the shore and on the right side."

"We can be positive of another thing—that boat definitely is headed for the dock. Can you make out the name of it?" Frank asked. Joe shook his head.

As the boat drew nearer, Frank read the name on its bow out loud. *"Sea . . . Mist. Sea Mist."*

Joe noticed that Frank was no longer looking at the boat but was trying to remember something.

"That's it!" Frank exclaimed. *"Sea Mist* was the name on the life preserver we found on the beach—one of the things that was taken out of the trunk of the MG!"

Chapter

7

THE *SEA MIST*, a large, oceangoing pleasure craft, glided in toward shore, closer and closer to the dock used by Bernhard Kruger. Then, about a hundred yards from the dock, it stopped.

"Looks like they're anchoring out there," Frank observed. "The flag's from Panama, but then a lot of American boats and ships have Panamanian registry."

"I can see someone on deck," Joe interrupted, looking through a pair of binoculars. "He's lowering a dinghy." The purring sound of the engines had now stopped. High rolling waves came in as the winds started to pick up just then.

"There's another guy," Frank said. He took

the field glasses from Joe. "They're going over the side. It looks like they're going to come ashore in the dinghy." He scanned the rest of the yacht with the binoculars. "I don't see anybody else on board." Dark clouds began passing in front of the sun, casting shadows over the scene. Frank watched as the men climbed into the dinghy and began rowing ashore. The dinghy swayed and bounced in the surf.

"The wind's starting to kick up a bit," Joe observed. "If there's a storm brewing, it probably means that no one will be taking the boat out again for a while."

"You've got that look on your face," Frank said. "Don't tell me. I know exactly what you're thinking."

"Well, look at it this way," said Joe through a broad grin. "The odds against getting blown up on two boats in two days are pretty high."

"Here we go, breaking and entering again. Just don't tell Chief Hodges."

Frank focused on the two men as they reached the dock. But the passing shadows made it difficult to see their features clearly. Neither guy would stand out in a crowd of other men in their late thirties or early forties. One had a well-trimmed, curly black beard. The other sported a knitted watch cap perched on the back of his head. Frank watched them as they pulled the dinghy out of the water and tied it securely to the dock.

They were close enough for Joe to see them clearly without the binoculars. "I tell you what," he said, "you keep tabs on those two, and *I'll* sneak aboard the boat alone. That way at least one of us will be following orders."

Frank sighed in agreement. "But we'll meet back here in thirty minutes." He watched as the two men from the boat walked up the beach to Kruger's door. "I'll make a dash for the house. As soon as they're being let in, I'll go over the wall. Less chance of someone looking out the window right then."

"Okay . . . now!" Joe said, seeing the door open.

"Thirty minutes," Frank reminded his brother. Then he broke into a sprint.

Joe slipped into a pair of trunks and then swam out to the boat. The water was choppy, and Joe found it easier to swim underwater as much as possible; that way he avoided the crashing waves above him. Swimming came naturally to him, and in very little time he'd reached the *Sea Mist*. He swam around to the stern of the boat so he wouldn't be seen boarding her if anyone happened to be looking out of Kruger's villa. Straining upward, he was able to grab hold of a rail and hoist himself onto the deck. The wind had picked up now, and the water slapped against the sides of the ship in regular bursts.

Joe took a moment to get his sea legs, steadying himself against the rail as the boat bounced and tipped. Then he walked forward along the deck, into a passageway that ran down the middle of the boat. The second door on the right was marked *Captain*. He opened it and looked in.

The first thing he noticed was a table full of papers against the right-hand wall. He checked the rest of the room—a bunk on his right, a little sink on the left, metal lockers across from him. Then he went inside. Maps and charts for all the waters and islands from Puerto Rico to Bermuda were strewn on the tabletop. Pencil markings on the maps showed that somebody was more interested in staying within the cover of little islands than taking more direct open-water routes. He left the chart table and walked across the cabin to a small desk beside the captain's locker.

Joe sifted quickly through the haphazard piles on the captain's desktop. "Notes, papers, checkbook stubs, computer disks—" Then he looked in the drawers beneath. "And here we have"—he opened a medium-size file—"a stash of blank credit cards. Jackpot!"

He had just picked up one of the blank cards when he heard noises above him on deck. He froze for a second, listening intently as the sounds became distinct—footsteps! There was a crew member on board—probably left behind to look after the boat. Joe was annoyed at himself for taking it for granted that the boat was deserted. But he had worse problems.

The footsteps were coming right toward the captain's cabin! Joe grabbed the check stubs and one of the disks on the desk and crammed it into the waist of his trunks. Then he made a dash for the cabin door—just as it began to open.

Joe pressed himself against the bulkhead behind the door as a tall, muscular man stepped into the room. His hair was cropped close, and the back of his neck was all lines and wrinkles. Joe stiffened, but the man never noticed him, going straight for the desk. He leaned over, his back to Joe, and opened the bottom drawer.

The boat was still swaying from the turbulence, and the cabin door was swinging on its hinges. Joe knew that if the door slammed shut, or if the tall man turned around, he'd be a goner. His only chance was to slip out right then. He stepped around the door and soundlessly backed out the open doorway, his eyes fixed on the big man.

The burly guy closed the desk drawer and stood up. Now! Joe told himself, turning to bolt.

Then he froze, staring at a short, broad, powerfully built man who gave him a nasty stare back.

"Hey, Mickey! We've got company." The stocky man's voice was a growl as he shouted to his partner in the cabin. His dark blue turtleneck sweater made it difficult to tell whether or not the squat man really did have a neck. But he definitely had a four-inch black switchblade handle in his hand. At the touch of a button, the handle sprouted a four-inch silver blade.

If Joe hadn't stopped short of the gravelly-voiced thug, he might have bowled him over and had a chance of getting away. Now he was trapped between Mr. Big and Mr. Broad. Moving back into the cabin meant four walls and the guy called Mickey; moving forward meant the man with the knife, but beyond him was the ocean. Joe decided to take a chance on getting past that switchblade.

The armed man had a two-inch gash across his left cheek, which told Joe this was definitely not the thug's first knife fight. And even though Joe stared into the man's eyes, he could see the extended right hand moving back and forth in front of his body with the shiny knife.

Then the muscleman made his move, lunging forward, the length of his right arm extended by four inches of sharp metal. His move was quick, narrowly missing Joe. The blade actually sliced his shirt as he twisted aside. But Joe had more than evasion in mind. Now his adversary was off-balance, leaning forward on one foot with his right hand out, his fist clenched tightly around the knife.

With the back of his left hand, Joe swung at the raised arm of his assailant. Then Joe quickly turned his body so that his right shoulder pinned the man's arm against the bulkhead until he dropped the knife. Joe's back was to the squat guy, who had grabbed Joe around the neck. Joe drew his elbow back, hard, and hit his target—the man's stomach.

"What the—" Mickey exclaimed as he stepped out of the cabin. "Hang on, Croaker!"

"Great name." Joe grinned as he backed up and slammed Croaker into the bulkhead. He could hear the thud as Croaker's head made contact with the metal. Croaker finally let go of his stranglehold around Joe's neck.

Joe backpedaled as he watched the man called Mickey move toward him now.

Mickey didn't look much more attractive from the front than he had from behind. He looked as if he shaved his head rather than cut his hair. And his eyebrows, which were also short, met just above his long, crooked nose.

The big guy was undoubtedly strong but slow

on his feet. And the rolling motion of the boat didn't help him.

Croaker, who was on his knees, reached out and wrapped his arms around Joe's left leg as Joe turned to race away from Mickey. Joe tried to shake him off, but Croaker held fast. He kept Joe back just long enough for Mickey to reach them.

"Hey, tough guy," he heard Mickey say from behind. And then Joe felt a hard object slam into the back of his head. The world went red and hazy. Then a crashing blow connected a second time behind Joe's ear. He buckled, then sank into blackness.

A gallon of seawater thrown into his face brought Joe around.

"Are you awake now?" a raspy voice said. "Or would you like another drink?"

When Joe could focus, he saw Croaker standing above him with a bucket. Joe started to go for his rival, but couldn't move. His hands and feet were bound tightly. His body aches were capped by a throbbing pain in the back of his head. "Now what are you going to do?" he asked.

"I'm not sure," Croaker replied. "I wanted to cut you up for shark bait, but I'll let Mickey decide."

"Has he said anything?" the big man asked as he walked over.

"Nah, we were just talking about the fish."

"What were you looking for?" Mickey demanded, turning his attention to Joe.

"Nothing," Joe replied. "I thought this was someone else's boat."

Mickey kicked him in the side. "What were you looking for, I said?"

"Nothing—are you going to kick me again?"

"Forget him," Croaker growled. "Let's toss him."

Mickey persisted. "What were you looking for? Who are you working for?"

Joe knew that whether he talked or not, he wasn't going to get out of this one. "I told you," he said, "I got on your boat by mistake. I'm not looking for anything, and I don't work for anybody. I'm just a tourist."

"Aw, do what you want with him," Mickey told Croaker. "I've got stuff to take care of." He turned and walked away, leaving Joe in Croaker's hands.

"Well, well," the muscleman said, "I guess it's just you and me now." He flicked out his switchblade, pressing the blade under Joe's chin. "Nah, I don't want to dirty my good knife. I tell you what—you swam out here, right? I'll let you swim back."

He left for a minute and then came back with

a small anchor. "This ought to give you some exercise." He tied the anchor to Joe's waist. "You can do the *dog* paddle," he said, grinning. "But pretty soon you'll be a dead *duck*."

His laugh was more like a frog's croak as he picked up Joe and the fifty-pound anchor. With the strength of a champion weight lifter, he lifted Joe above his shoulders and tossed him into the ocean, like a fisherman throwing back an undersize fish.

Chapter

8

THE ANCHOR FASTENED around Joe's waist did its job perfectly. It sank rapidly to the twenty-five-foot ocean bottom, dragging Joe along like a fish on a line.

Every muscle ached as Joe tried to squirm free from the ropes that bound him. His head was throbbing. He tried to remain calm and conserve his oxygen. But his fear and his struggles caused his heart to race faster and faster, burning up precious oxygen.

He could feel the binding loosening around his legs, and he kept rubbing his feet together, trying to slip an ankle free. The wet rope stretched, and finally Joe did pull his legs loose. But his hands had been tied more firmly—they wouldn't budge. And no matter how hard he kicked his legs, it wasn't enough to overcome the weight attached to his waist. He was almost out of air.

Joe gritted his teeth, forcing his mouth shut so the water wouldn't rush in as he started to black out. Something rasped against his lips! A heavy stream of bubbles rose in front of his eyes. Someone was trying to force something into his mouth. It was Frank, trying to get him to take the regulator of his scuba tank. Joe opened his mouth and started breathing rapidly into the regulator, his teeth clamping down on the hard rubber mouthpiece. Frank stood by holding his breath, one hand on the regulator, the other on his brother's shoulder.

It seemed like an eternity before Joe pulled himself together enough to realize that he and his brother had to share the same regulator. He inhaled deeply, then motioned for Frank to take the mouthpiece back.

Frank took a deep breath, gave the regulator back to Joe, and then, using a knife he had tied to his weight belt, cut the ropes to the anchor. He and Joe started swimming slowly for the surface, sharing the oxygen supply on the way up. Frank cut the ropes that bound Joe's hands.

The Hardys surfaced. All around them the sky and water were black. The wind had blown in rain clouds and was tossing the waves violently against the boys. Joe threw his head back and sucked in the fresh air. A bullet whizzed past his ear.

"Down!" Frank said. The men on the boat must have seen the air bubbles from the scuba apparatus.

With only one tank between them, Joe's first impulse was to try to swim clear of the bullets. But he knew there was too great a chance of one of them being hit.

Like it or not, they had to return underwater to share the scuba mouthpiece. Although they were still close to the surface, the light made it difficult for the men on the boat to find their mark. The two brothers dived even deeper. A minute earlier the ocean depth meant danger—now it offered safety.

Even underwater the Hardys could hear the *zing* of bullets cutting through the waves, but they were far out of range. The storm was blowing in full fury now, and Frank and Joe knew their attackers would be unable to see them. They swam among the reefs, looking for a safe spot behind rocks where they could crawl back onto land.

After they pulled themselves up on the rocks they lay back for a moment, catching their breath. The waves were crashing against the rocks, covering them with spray and filling the air with a sound that was almost hypnotic.

Frank unhooked himself from his gear and said, "That was close. Do you need a minute more to rest?"

"No, I'm okay," Joe responded. He coughed a few times, then got to his feet. "We better split. They'll come for us and the rain's going to start any second."

As they climbed over the slippery rocks, Frank explained why he had swum out to the boat with the scuba gear. "I could hear the men talking inside the house. They said something about the guys still on the boat. I knew you'd be in trouble, and I thought the best place for me to be was underwater by the boat. I returned to the car, and then—" He stopped short as the clouds finally released their load. Fat, pelting drops drove holes into the water and beat a steady, heavy rhythm against the rocks.

Frank ran his arm across his eyes to clear the view. "Look!" he exclaimed. "Back on the boat."

Frank and Joe watched through a sheet of rain. Mickey and Croaker began unloading ordinary-looking, tarp-covered boxes from the boat into a second dinghy. "Rain or no rain," Joe remarked, "it looks like they're going to get that boat unloaded—pronto."

"They probably figure that we can lead the cops back to them."

"Right. And if they do go on board, they don't want to get caught with the goods, whatever they are."

"It's got to be blank credit cards!" Joe told Frank how he'd found a drawer full of the blanks in the captain's cabin.

"Well, there's nothing more we can do. Let's get out of the rain," Frank suggested.

Joe laughed. "Don't tell me you're afraid of getting wet!"

The brothers found themselves laughing heartily as they headed back to Alicia's car. Then Joe's laughter stopped suddenly. "Wait a minute!" he said. "If the goons on board guess we made it back to shore, they'll call the house to let them know. Then the guys inside will be waiting for us—at the car."

"Right," Frank agreed. "We'd better separate and circle around in case it's being guarded."

As they were moving silently through the few trees that separated the rocky shore from the roadway the rain let up to a steady shower. They both reached the car about the same time. Everything seemed to be normal. No one was around.

"Put the gear in the trunk," Frank said, "while I get the car started." He shook himself off, climbed in, and started up the engine. Then he looked in the rearview mirror. The trunk was open, obliterating his view. He looked in the sideview mirror—to find the image of a familiar car. The BMW! Frank saw that the black car was heading straight for them. But Joe couldn't; his back was to the rapidly approaching car and the light rain was muffling the sound. He was a perfect target.

Frank moved like lightning. He shoved open the car door and stepped out, screaming, "Joe! Behind you! The car!"

Now Joe heard the racing engine at his back, and knew immediately what was happening. He reached into the trunk and yanked out the metal scuba tank; in one move he turned and hurled the heavy tank at the windshield of the black BMW.

The car was only ten feet away when the heavy tank crashed into the large windshield, creating a spider's web of cracks before breaking all the way through the glass. Joe was poised to dive into the mud on the side of the road, but his fast action and deadly aim had worked. The BMW screeched to a halt. The tank had landed in the lap of the driver. Joe saw his arms folded in front of his face, the knitted cap still perched on his head.

"Take off!" Joe shouted to his brother.

Frank knew what Joe had in mind. He jumped back in the car, put it into gear, and stepped on the gas. Just before the car sped off, he felt Joe thumping into the trunk. It all happened so fast, and the little car squealed so noisily as it peeled out, that Frank didn't even know if they were being shot at or not.

He looked into the sideview mirror and saw one man scramble out of the passenger side of the BMW. He knew the pursuit was over—for now. He kept watching the mirror until the man, too small to identify, became a tiny speck. Once the coast was clear, Frank stopped to give Joe a chance to get out of the trunk. "Want to ride up front?" he asked.

Joe climbed out of the trunk, stretching his arms. "I was just starting to enjoy the view from the rear." He grinned.

"Did you learn anything else at Kruger's?" Joe asked as they drove back to Hamilton under the now clearing sky.

"When I got up to the side of the house, I stood under an open window. One of the guys from the yacht was called Gus, and the other Del—I think he was the one that you nailed with the scuba tank. Anyway, the first thing out of Gus's mouth was something about the other two guys on the boat. We didn't figure there was anybody else left. I didn't know what to do. I wanted to stay and listen to Kruger, but I was afraid that you were headed for trouble. So I sneaked back to the car, grabbed the gear, and headed out."

It was two-thirty when the Hardys got back to Hamilton. Joe suggested they stop at the police station to get the ballistics report on Alfred Montague's gun and to find out how Walt Conway was doing.

"Hello, Chief Boulton," the brothers said as they entered his office.

"Hi, boys." The chief looked the boys up and down, almost hesitant to ask about their damp attire. They had quickly pulled their jeans on over their wet trunks. "How's the crime-fighting business?"

Frank and Joe exchanged a look. Joe spoke first and then they both filled the chief in on the specifics of what they discovered at Kruger's house.

"How's Conway?" Frank asked.

"He's recovering quite well," the chief responded. "And I suppose you want to know about the report on the gun you brought in?"

Frank and Joe just nodded.

"Well, Montague's gun was *not* the gun used to shoot Conway—or anybody else that we know of, for that matter."

"That's a relief." Joe sighed.

"One curious thing, though," Chief Boulton added. "Joe's fingerprints were the *only* prints on that gun. Before he handled it, it had been wiped clean!" He pulled the gun out of his drawer and handed it back to Joe.

Joe screwed up his face, puzzled. "The gun had been fired, but why would someone wipe the prints off?"

The chief just shrugged.

Joe leaned against the wall, trying to figure it out. "Wait a minute! I completely forgot!"

"You mean you know why the gun was wiped clean?" Frank asked.

"No," he said as though he couldn't care less about it. "I forgot the stuff I took from the boat!" He pulled something from the waist-band of his trunks that looked like a soggy piece of paper on a square plate and tossed it on the table, a wide grin on his face. "Check stubs and a disk, from the *Sea Mist*."

Chapter

9

FRANK AND JOE took the check stubs and computer disk with them, certain that some information could be retrieved. They wanted to check them over carefully when they got back to Montague's house and could use his computer.

There were things bothering them—little unresolved things—including why Montague's gun was wiped clean of fingerprints. Why had his credit card turned up on the cliff overlooking the wreck of the MG? And the larger questions, such as, what happened the evening Montague was supposedly kidnapped, and was he holding back anything? There were so many unanswered questions—and so little time left.

"We've spent the past two days getting

bruised and battered and out of breath." Joe sagged back in his seat as the brothers headed for home.

"But we're not even close to solving this case," Frank said. "And if we don't by tomorrow, we won't deserve a vacation."

Joe scowled. "All we have are names, some pictures, and a good idea who's behind the credit card scam and trying to kill us off."

"Maybe Montague can help," Frank suggested.

"Montague?"

Frank shrugged. "He's either for us or against us. If he's *for* us, then maybe we can get him to help in solving this thing. If he's *against* us, then it's time we confronted him and forced his hand."

"Okay, here's your chance." Joe cocked his head, indicating that they were back at Montague's house.

"I didn't realize we were home yet," Frank said, surprised.

"That worries me," Joe mused, "considering *you're* driving."

They parked Alicia's car and headed for the house.

"Oh," said Frank, remembering something. "We should get the stuff out of the trunk."

"The only thing in the trunk was *me;* the scuba gear's in the front seat of the BMW."

"But what about the second tank?"

"Oh. Guess you missed that. I threw it at the front tire of the BMW after I got in the trunk. There wasn't enough room in there for the two of us, and it looked like a good way to slow them down when they chased us."

"But they didn't chase us," Frank reminded his brother.

"Maybe the tank under the tire worked!" Joe said with a big grin on his face.

Montague and Alicia had come to the front door to greet them.

"Hello!" they both said.

The brothers said "Hi" as they walked up to the door. Then Joe added another "Hi!" and a broad smile as he looked at Alicia.

They were ushered into the living room, Montague and his daughter anxious to hear how the day had gone so far.

Joe started in without even waiting to sit down. He was uncomfortable pretending to be the friendly guest while he still had doubts about his host. "There are some things we have to talk about." He thought it sounded unusually cold and began to feel even more uncomfortable when he noticed Alicia staring at him, a look of worry on her face.

"Yes, I know," Montague said without hesitating. His manner was relaxed and friendly, and it helped ease the tension. "There's some-

thing I have to tell you boys first. Sit down."
He motioned for the brothers to have a seat on
the couch as he sat down on an easy chair
opposite them. Alicia grabbed a cushion from
the couch and sat on the floor.

Frank and Joe listened to what started like a
confession.

"I know more than you think about this
Kruger affair," Montague began. "And I'm
not exactly a retired copper."

Frank watched as Joe fidgeted in his seat.
Alicia looked up at the younger Hardy, but for
the first time since their arrival at the villa
almost a week earlier, Joe was unaware of her
presence.

"I wasn't able to say anything until now,"
Montague continued. "In fact, even Alicia
didn't know all the details until this morning."
He paused, looking from Frank to Joe. "I'm
only semiretired, and I'm not really a detective. I work for British Intelligence. And for
the last month, I've been on loan to your FBI."

Joe sat still, staring at Montague. Of all the
confessions he'd been preparing himself for,
this was the one he least expected. Frank
smiled broadly, with a look that showed he was
eager to hear more.

"You see," Montague resumed, "the FBI
knows of my work with British Intelligence,

and I'm the only agent who's an established local."

"And the government here? Do they know about you?" Frank asked.

Montague nodded. "They're aware—unofficially. The Bermuda police haven't made any progress on the activities of Kruger's group, especially since the consequences of his actions are felt primarily *outside* of Bermuda, particularly in your country. The credit card distribution scam is operating mostly in the United States. But the FBI is more interested in where the credit card blanks are stamped than they are with the distribution. If they close down the counterfeiting operation, then the distribution stops."

"Then you've been working on this case all along," Frank stated.

"Yes, but I wasn't allowed to tell Alicia or you until today. Even Alicia thought I could be involved with Kruger in some way!"

Frank turned to Alicia. *"You're* the one who wiped the fingerprints off your father's gun."

Alicia gave an embarrassed nod. "I was in such a state that I didn't know what to do. Dad was so suspicious, so secretive. When I heard that a Bermuda policeman had been shot, I really got nervous. I knew Dad kept a gun. It was always in the study and always spotlessly clean. When I saw it had been fired, I didn't know what to think."

"I had practiced with the gun on Tuesday," Montague interrupted. "Simple as that."

"So I wiped the prints off the gun." Alicia looked down, the beginnings of a blush rising to her cheeks. "It was a rather stupid thing to do."

Joe gave her a sheepish grin. He took the revolver out of his back pocket and placed it on the end table. "Welcome to the club," he said. "You weren't the only one who thought your father might be working with Kruger. Remember that credit card we found?"

"Only too well," Montague said. "I knew you boys had your suspicions then, especially when you never told me where you found the card."

"At the scene of the crime," Joe said and raised an eyebrow. Then he laughed at himself. "It was right where our car—uh, *your* car— was forced off the road."

"Ah." Montague nodded, thinking. "So, Kruger planned it so I was to be your primary suspect. You see, Kruger doesn't know I'm with British Intelligence, or that I'm involved with this case in any way. However, he knew about you and your investigation, and some-how you must have worried him. He decided to arrange an 'accident.' But you boys surprised him—you survived.

"So he had to try a bigger production—a bomb on board *One Blue Vista*. A murder, complete with someone to blame. Kruger expected you to be eliminated. And he thoughtfully supplied the police with a suspect." He tapped his finger lightly against his chest. "Me. I was the only choice since you boys had no connection with anyone else on the island, and since he made sure I had no alibi."

"Then the whole bit with Martin Powers was a setup, too," Joe suggested.

"Right. I was lured out of the house under the pretext that your lives were in danger."

"They were!" Joe interrupted.

"Yes, but the idea was to keep me out of sight during that time so I would have no alibi. Then you boys were led to believe that I was on Powers's boat. Kruger knew that once you got to the boat and found out that no one was on board, you wouldn't pass up the chance to search it. You were supposed to go out in a blaze of glory."

Alicia picked up a newspaper. "I guess you must have missed today's *Nassau Guardian*." She held up the front page. "You two really look cute!"

Joe grimaced and Frank laughed as the two of them looked at the photo of Joe on the front page. It showed the fire in the background, while up front was a furious, soggy, handcuffed Joe with his mouth wide open. "That must have been taken when I was yelling for the police to arrest Kruger instead of us," he said.

"Well, here's a picture of Powers being interviewed, safe and sound—and not dead, as Kruger said. And here we are, *still damp*," Frank said.

Joe stood up and reached into his pants pocket to pull out the wad of soggy paper and the computer disk. "I took this from the boat this morning," he said, directing himself to Montague.

"What is it?" Montague asked.

"A checkbook—I mean, the stubs that were attached to checks—and a computer disk."

"Now all we need is an underwater computer so we can read the disk." Frank grinned. "And the ink on the check stubs has all washed out."

"We won't be able to read the check stubs," Montague cut in, "but we may be able to retrieve some information from the disk. Why don't you boys go up and change, and Alicia and I'll work on it."

When Frank returned, he found Alicia and her father at work on a computer in the library. A bottle of cleaning material, some swabs, and a hair dryer sat on the desk, along with tweezers and a knife. Sunlight was dazzling the cozy room. All was quiet, except for the whining and clicking of the computer.

"We've cleaned and dried the disk," Alicia explained, "but a lot of the data has been lost."

Joe appeared and looked at the computer screen. "Looks like you're breaking a code."

"We're using a program that will fill in some of the missing information by running through plausible letter and word combinations," Montague explained. "There are still a lot of complete words or names missing, but at least we can make some sense of it."

He pointed to the top of the screen. "The disk is titled 'The Number File.' It contains hundreds of names, addresses—"

"And credit card numbers," Joe said, staring at the flickering columns. "Some of the entries even include a listing for 'mother's maiden name'!"

"They're all real people, and real card numbers," Frank explained. "That's one of the things that's making it so hard to crack this case—the crooks are using real credit card numbers—like a second card. None of the numbers are phony."

"But how do they get the numbers?" Joe wanted to know.

"I think it's possible for someone to tap into

a company's computer line and retrieve information without removing it from where it's stored," said Frank. "Something like going into an office and reading files without taking the files out of the office."

"It's a new kind of theft," added Montague. "They're stealing *information* rather than goods. It makes it a much harder crime to crack."

"I guess we should pass this information on to Boulton," Frank suggested.

"I'll take care of it," Montague said. He dialed the phone next to him. After a pause, "Hello, Chief Boulton, please. This is Alfred Mont—Hello—Hello!" He clicked the button up and down. "The line's gone dead."

"Could have been the storm." Alicia sounded as if she wanted that to be the reason.

"Sure." Joe quickly agreed to keep her from getting anxious. "Must have been the storm."

"I still think we should take a copy of this disk to Chief Boulton," Frank said. "Will you and Alicia be okay here alone?"

"Sure," Montague replied. "I've got the revolver, remember?" He slipped another disk into the computer and hit some keys. "Here's a copy. In the meantime I'll try to clean up some more information from the original."

"Since the rain has stopped," Joe said, "we

can take the mopeds. You two can have the car in case anything happens.

"Fine," Montague agreed.

They said their goodbyes, and once again the two brothers were on the road, headed for Hamilton.

Not five minutes from the Montagues' villa Frank saw the all-too-familiar black BMW in his rearview mirror. A piece of lightweight plastic had been secured over the hole in the windshield.

"Joe," he shouted over the roar of the two bikes, "we've got company!"

Joe looked over his shoulder. "I guess they cut the phone lines just to get us out of the house." He let out the throttle on his bike.

Frank couldn't hear his reply over the roar of the two bikes going full out. But at a top speed of fifty miles per hour, they were no match for the BMW. The boys were exposed and defenseless on their bikes.

The strip of road they were driving along was narrow, with no place to turn off. They were riding single file now, Frank's bike faltering a little and lagging behind.

Frank looked over his shoulder and saw that the BMW had closed the distance between them to less than fifty feet. He leaned over the front of the bike to cut wind resistance and to make himself a smaller target for the bullets he expected would be flying at him.

He didn't expect what did happen. The car, going at least thirty miles an hour faster than the bike, rammed into the back of Frank's moped. The bike flipped. And suddenly Frank found himself spinning in midair, flying over the top of the speeding BMW.

Chapter

10

Joe cringed as he heard the sickening crash of his brother's bike flipping over again and again until it bounced off the highway and stopped. He turned in time to see the black car come to a halt. He jammed on his brakes, leaned far to the right, and turned the bike 180 degrees. He twisted the throttle, downshifted, popped the clutch, and lurched forward in the direction of the crumpled bike.

Then he noticed his brother, who was lying motionless in a large bush by the side of the road about forty feet behind the BMW. Mickey and Croaker had gotten out of the car and were sauntering over to Frank's body.

"Hold it!" Joe yelled in rage as he sped toward them.

"I knew we wouldn't have to go after you!" Mickey shouted. "You'd come back for what's left of this guy." He lifted Frank behind the legs, and Croaker was ready to take his arms.

Joe drove right up to the two men, flying off his bike and landing on Mickey like a rodeo star in a bulldogging contest. His bike went sailing past them. It leaned over until it fell to the pavement, sending sparks everywhere and sliding off the side of the road. Mickey hit the ground hard. Joe lashed out with his fist and caught him with a blow to the jaw. Then he spun around as Croaker was about to grab him from behind. He threw a right into the short thug's midsection. His arm was back, ready to land a knockout blow when someone grabbed his arm.

"I got him, Del," his new attacker announced.

"Nice work, Gus." The two thugs had joined Mickey and Croaker. As Joe struggled to break the hold on his arm, he remembered those two names. Frank had said they were back at Kruger's. With a desperate yank, Joe pulled free— just in time for Del to put a chokehold on him.

"For old times," Gus said, lashing out and punching Joe in the stomach—knocking all the air and fight out of him.

"Lock him in the trunk before I kill him," Croaker ordered as he got up off the ground, his voice even gruffer than usual. "And hide the bikes." He pointed to a small clump of greenery near where Frank's bike had landed. "This time the Hardys are going to disappear without a trace!"

"What about this one?" Mickey asked, standing over Frank's body.

"Throw him in the back seat. He won't give you any trouble—he's dead!"

Joe tried to look over his shoulder at his brother as Mickey opened the trunk. Gus spun him around, and Joe twisted frantically, struggling to see.

"I've had enough of this," Croaker growled as he placed his hand against a nerve on Joe's neck. Joe collapsed, unconscious.

When Joe awoke, his stomach ached, and his shoulder felt as if it had been stepped on. His head was swimming. And he was rocking back and forth, back and forth. Then all at once he knew the rocking wasn't in his imagination. He was on a boat, thrown in the bilge. Looking at the emptiness of his surroundings, he thought about Frank then for the first time.

Before he could go over what had happened, or try to figure out what was about to happen, a door opened on the other side of the room. Joe recognized Mickey. "Enjoy your trip!"

The thug cackled as he shoved a body into the room with Joe.

"Frank!" Joe yelled. In spite of the fact that his older brother was bruised, bloodied, and dazed, he'd never looked more welcome to Joe. "I thought you were dead!"

"I know" were Frank's first words. "Mickey was gloating about the way Croaker announced I was dead. That was Croaker's idea of a joke. He knew I hadn't been killed, but he was trying to get to you."

"He's a real piece of work—" Joe swallowed the rest of his words. "But you're okay?"

"I'll live, maybe." Frank forced a grim smile. He said he was black and blue, and his body hurt all over. "They said they didn't want me to die before they had a chance to kill me properly." He looked at his brother. "*You* all right?"

"Yeah. I wasn't hurt or anything. I was just given a nice, long nap." He paused, running his teeth over his lower lip. "Well, what do we do now?"

"I don't know," Frank admitted. "I checked out this room thoroughly before they brought me topside for a few questions. Did you see what's in those boxes?"

"No." Joe shook his head, still a little groggy. "I just got here." He got up and walked over to one of the boxes his brother had pointed out. "Wha-do-ya-know!" he said as he pulled out a handful of bright new credit cards, all stamped with names and account numbers.

"And all the other boxes are filled with the same," Frank informed Joe, pointing out the other ten or so boxes that were scattered throughout the room. "There wasn't enough time to stamp the load of credit card blanks you found on the *Sea Mist* earlier. So this is probably the delivery we were supposed to get Dad the information about."

"Well, we're certainly right on top of things." Joe scratched the back of his neck. "If the *Sea Mist* did come from Puerto Rico, like it showed on the maps I saw, then the boat brings in a load of blanks from there, drops them at Kruger's, and then takes a load of stamped cards wherever we're going now."

"Yeah," Frank added. "Wherever."

"Any ideas?" Joe asked.

"Feels like we're on the open seas, and when I was topside I saw we were headed right into the setting sun, so we're either going due west or southwest."

"Are we on the *Sea Mist?*" Joe asked.

"Couldn't tell. The only close-up look I ever got of the *Sea Mist* was from underwater. I'd guess from the way she rides that she's about a sixty-four-footer."

"We must be headed to the U.S. mainland, though," Joe figured.

"Quite right, boys!" Mickey had opened the door just in time to catch Joe's remark. "But you won't see the mainland again. We have a scientific project in mind for you. You're going to get a firsthand look at how things—and people—disappear in the Bermuda Triangle!" Mickey let out a sinister laugh as he gave the brothers time to understand what he meant.

Joe hated Croaker, but he liked Mickey even less. He slowly started to move away from Frank. Maybe while Mickey's attention was centered on one of the brothers, the other could somehow overcome him.

A revolver appeared in Mickey's hand. "You keep moving like that," he said to Joe, "and you're never going to hear the end of my story."

Joe froze while Mickey continued. "You've caused us a lot of trouble. We even had to send a diver down to fetch your camera from that MG, in case you happened to get a picture of the boat. And we got a bonus—the life preserver! I didn't even know that was missing."

He grinned at them nastily. "Too bad you didn't hold on to it. You'd find it handy where you're going. Before we rendezvous tomorrow with some friends, we're dumping you overboard. This time we'll *know* there's no chance you'll show up again. And without any bodies, the police can't be sure of a crime." His laugh echoed off the bare walls. "And the final joke is that we'll buy a couple of thousand dollars' worth of merchandise in *your* names with *your* credit cards before anybody even knows you're missing!"

He looked crazed as he backed out of the room and stopped suddenly in the doorway. "I almost forgot. They say bad things happen in threes. Well, tomorrow by this time there'll be three of you sharing an ocean grave."

The sound of the slamming door echoed throughout the room until it was finally muted by the sound of rushing water outside the bulkhead. Joe and Frank looked at each other without speaking. There was one light in the dim room—a bare bulb hanging from the ceiling attached to a long cord plugged into the far wall. There wasn't much they could use to escape and overcome their captors.

Frank was the first to break the silence. "Who do you suppose the other person is?"

Joe's face was tight. "Think about it. Who else do we know who's working on this case? Montague!"

As if on cue, the door opened again, and someone was shoved into the room. "Company!" a voice yelled out. Frank and Joe watched as the person stumbled into the light.

"Alicia!" they shouted simultaneously. Joe rushed up to her and grabbed her by the shoulders. Her eyes were red, her face pale, but she didn't seem to be hurt. "Did they—"

"I'm fine," she interrupted. Her smile assured the brothers that she was okay.

"What happened? How did you get here?" Frank asked.

"After you left, I started wondering about the phone line. At first I thought maybe it had been cut to trap us in the house. *Then* I wondered if Kruger's plan was to get both of you *out* of the house.

"You couldn't go very fast on those bikes. I decided to follow you in the car in case you needed to get away quickly. Dad said he'd wait at home in case something happened and we missed one another.

"I practically rammed into that black BMW you had told me about, and then I saw your bikes. But I didn't see either of you. I tried to turn around, but before I could get out of there, the passenger door swung open, and this big guy turned off the ignition key and grabbed me.

"They forced me into their car and asked me a lot of questions. I didn't say anything, so then they took me with them. They questioned me topside, and when I wouldn't tell them anything again, they brought me down here."

"I'm glad to see you, but I'm unhappy that you're here," Joe burst out. "Does that make any sense?"

Alicia grinned. "I understand."

"They didn't try any rough stuff?" Frank asked in a soft, concerned voice.

"No—they didn't even search me." Alicia's grin grew wider as she reached behind her. "I've had this all along." She pulled something out from her baggy jeans.

"The revolver!" Joe stared in amazement.

"Dad said I should take it just in case."

"Fantastic! Let's invite Mickey back in here, threaten him with the gun, and then take over the ship," Joe said.

"Not so fast," Frank cautioned. "If Mickey forces us to use this gun, that would warn the others. Besides, remember what Mickey said about a rendezvous tomorrow. We need to find out where that meeting is."

"But they're going to dispose of us *before* then."

"Look. There's no way we can reach Florida by tomorrow, so the rendezvous must be at sea."

"We've got to figure out where the rendezvous is, and *then* find a way out of this mess.

It shouldn't be too difficult to pick the lock on this door—the only real problem is how to overcome the crew."

"Are there just the four of them?" Joe asked.

"I only saw two," Frank answered.

"There are three," Alicia confirmed. "The short, fat guy with the funny voice stayed behind."

"Croaker," Joe said. "Did you happen to notice the name of the boat?" he asked excitedly.

"The *Sea Mist*."

"Great. Then I know how to get to the wheelhouse and the captain's cabin."

"Good," Frank said, feeling more confident now. "Tonight the boat will probably be on automatic pilot, and we'll know the direction of the ship. Picture that as a straight line from Bermuda to someplace on the U.S. mainland—"

"But you said we won't reach the mainland," Joe interrupted.

"That's not the important thing," Frank said. "If one of us can get to the wheelhouse and reset the pilot—heading us off course—we'll be able to find the rendezvous point."

"How?" Joe wanted to know.

Frank drew a line in the dust on the floor with his finger. "Let's say this is the original route." He ran his finger partway along the same line, then turned off at an angle. "Here's where we turn the ship during the night." He extended the line.

"But tomorrow morning they'll discover they're miles off course," Joe said.

Alicia chimed in, understanding Frank's plan, "And they'll have to plot a new direction. And where that course crosses the original course is where the rendezvous is set."

As Alicia spoke, Frank drew a new line that intersected the first. "X marks the spot!"

"It's a big triangle," Joe said.

"That's why it's called the triangulation method. It's really nothing more than geometry."

"Once we know where the meeting place is," Frank added, "we can contact the authorities and head back to Bermuda. Got it?"

"Got it!"

The three were not interrupted again as they sat quietly and discussed their plans. No one had even brought them any food. It was after five when Frank said it was time to move. He picked the lock on the door in about fifteen minutes, using the wire from one of Alicia's barrettes. Joe crept out and found his way up to the wheelhouse. Everyone was asleep, and he wasn't seen. The wheelhouse was empty, and Joe had no trouble setting the automatic pilot for a different course. He then returned to their prison.

"Done," he said when he reentered the room.

"Any problems?" Frank asked.

"The only problem I had was coming back here without going after those hoods. It seems crazy not to take care of them now that we're free."

"We need to know that rendezvous point," Frank emphasized once again. "We're too tired to think clearly now anyway—let's get some sleep. Then we'll figure out a plan in the morning before anyone comes back."

There was nothing to do now *except* wait. The three captives flattened out some boxes to lie on. Joe took the revolver from Alicia and slipped it under one of the boxes. Then they all huddled together on their hard, makeshift bunks and went to sleep.

The sharp sound of a piercing alarm woke them a couple of hours later. "What's that?" Alicia asked, startled.

"The radar warning system," Frank informed them. "It probably means there's something in the boat's path. It's a warning to the captain to take the boat off automatic pilot and steer a new course."

"Then they'll find out the automatic pilot has been tampered with."

"Let's see—" Frank looked at his watch. "It's almost seven A.M. We've gone far enough off course to calculate the rendezvous point once they set the new course."

The alarm stopped, and the trio could feel the boat turn sharply to port. Then, without warning, the door to the room was unlocked and slammed into the bulkhead.

Mickey burst into the room, gun in hand. "So, somebody was playing captain in the middle of the night, huh? Did you really think that if you set a course for the Carolinas, the boat would reach land before we got up in the morning?"

Joe was searching for the gun he had taken from Alicia a few hours earlier, but it had slipped under one of the box flaps. He started to reach for it.

"You! Tough guy!" Mickey said, looking at Joe. "Stand up!"

Joe got slowly to his feet as Gus and Del stalked in.

"Over against that wall. Gus, tie him up. Now you, handsome," he said, nodding at Frank. "Stand up, turn around, and put your hands behind your back. Del, take care of him."

"I'll take care of him, all right."

"Just tie him up—that's all."

"Why don't we just toss them overboard right now?" Gus asked.

"Because we want to wait for local radio contact with the other ship. What if the FBI found out our rendezvous point, and our boys aren't there but the Coast Guard is? We might need some bargaining power."

Frank and Joe were securely tied with rope, then thrown down on the deck like sacks of potatoes. Then, after Gus and Del left, Mickey went over to Alicia, grabbed her by the arm, and pulled her toward the door.

"We'll take care of your girlfriend, lover boy. The next time you see her, you'll both be twelve thousand feet underwater!"

Chapter

11

"A FINE MESS your plan has gotten us into," Joe grumbled. "I should have nailed them all last night when I had the chance."

"Stop griping and try to get out of your ropes," Frank said, cutting him off. "We haven't got much time."

"They tied me so tight I can't move anything except my fingers."

"Good. Then get your fingers over here and try to loosen *my* ropes."

Joe rolled across the room, mumbling. "Is—won—irks—mooss."

"What?"

"I said, this only works in the movies."

"It'd better work now," Frank said. "Or we'll never see another movie."

The two brothers rolled and kicked until they were lying back to back. Joe tried to slip his fingers into the knot that secured Frank's hands.

"It's no use," he said, his voice showing as much anger as frustration. "These guys are all seamen. That's a sailor's knot. I can't work it loose."

"Wait a minute," Frank said. "I think Del's the pilot, and Mickey's a sailor, but I don't know about Gus. He's the one who tied you. Let's see if I can loosen *your* knot."

Frank maneuvered until his fingers could grasp the main knot that bound Joe's hands. "It's just a lot of loops, I think. If I pull on it near the end, I think I can open one loop at a time." Frank struggled to undo Joe's bonds bit by bit.

"There," he exclaimed, his fingers raw, "that should do it. Open your fist and slip your right hand up."

Joe turned and twisted, and the ropes burned into his wrist. "Got it!" he whispered triumphantly as his hand came free. Thirty seconds later he was standing, a coil of rope on the deck beside his feet.

He leaned over and untied the sailor's knots that held Joe. "Even with two hands this knot is hard to undo," he remarked. "There! Now to find the gun."

Joe searched for the gun under the broken boxes while Frank shook himself loose from his ropes.

"It's not here!" Joe shoved the credit card boxes across the deck.

"It's got to be," Frank insisted as he joined in the search. "Where was it?"

"Right here under a box, next to Alicia and me."

"Alicia!" Frank figured that must be the answer. "When Mickey ordered you to stand up, Alicia was still sitting. She probably took the gun."

"Great. Now who's going to rescue who?" Joe muttered. "We've got to get out of here. I hope Alicia doesn't try anything foolish."

"Maybe she can get the drop on them."

"And maybe not." Joe's voice was grim.

Frank hurried over to the door and tried the handle. "It's open!" He peered out, then stuck his head back in and closed the door. "There's no place to hide between here and the upper deck. If we get spotted, we're done for. Unless we get a gun."

Joe shook his head. "I'm sure they're not going to send Alicia down here with hers! They didn't bring us anything to eat yesterday, so I doubt they'll come this morning—except to dispose of us."

"Then we have to *coax* someone down

here," Frank suggested. "If we make a commotion—"

"And then one of us hides behind the door and bops them when they come in? I don't think so. That's a good way to get shot. No one's going to open that door more than an inch until they see us still tied up on the other side of the room."

"I have an idea," Frank said. "Help me get that light bulb down." Frank clasped his hands together to give him a foot up. Joe unhooked a spool of wire that was hung over a nail in one of the beams.

"What are you going to do with a light bulb?" Joe asked.

"Not the bulb—the wire. The cord is long enough to stretch from the wall outlet to the door. If we remove the wires from the socket and attach them to the inside metal doorknob and plug it in, anyone touching the outside knob will get a shock."

"But it won't be enough to knock anyone out," Joe pointed out.

"The ship is two-twenty volts, and that should stun him long enough for us to make a move. We just have to hope that only one guy comes down."

Joe was still not convinced. "And what'll we use to cut the wires?"

"I still have my watch. I can smash the

crystal, and use the broken glass.'' Frank un-
buckled his watch strap and rammed the watch
face against the deck until the glass cover
cracked. He picked up a large piece and held
it.

"Sounds good—except for one thing: once
we start working on this, we'll have no light.
It'll be pitch-black in here."

"Can't have things too easy," Frank said.
"Now get your bearings—remember where
everything is. Ready?" He pulled the plug, and
the room was plunged into darkness.

A half hour later, at eight-thirty A.M., the
men could hear a faint banging sound coming
from the hold.

"Gus, check our guests," Del ordered. "If
they've gotten loose, knock them out! I've had
enough of those two."

"All right." Gus walked below to the room
that held the two captives. He pulled his gun
and started to turn the doorknob.

"Now!" Joe whispered.

Frank was ready. He pushed the wire into
the socket, and the Hardys heard a muffled
shriek followed by the sound of Gus hitting the
deck.

Gus had been prepared for what the brothers
might have tried after he got into the room, but
he never expected anything before he even got

the door open. Joe sprang into action, jerking the cord free, swinging open the door, and throwing a fist into Gus's jaw almost in one move. The shot to the mouth kept the muscle-bound thug from shouting out.

Frank was in the doorway now, and with one karate chop to the back of Gus's neck, Gus slumped to the floor.

"We've got to work fast, before they decide he's been gone too long," Frank advised. He dragged the body into the darkened room while Joe picked up some of the rope that had been used to tie them. He fashioned a gag out of part of Gus's shirt, and in no time the thug was bound so securely it would take machetes to cut him free. "Now, *those* are sailor's knots!" Frank said to the still-unconscious Gus.

Joe picked up Gus's gun from the passage-way. "Let's do it," he said to Frank.

The two brothers sneaked along the passage-way and up the stairs onto the main deck. They tiptoed past the captain's cabin, checking to see if it was occupied.

"They're probably all in the pilothouse," Frank whispered.

"There's only two of them and two of us now," Joe reminded his brother.

"But we have to be careful Alicia doesn't get caught in the middle," Frank said cautiously. Joe nodded in quick agreement.

The two brothers made their way to the wheelhouse without being seen. Del and Mickey sat in the middle of the room, laughing and joking. Alicia was on a stool directly inside the open doorway.

Frank and Joe rushed the wheelhouse, Joe's gun drawn. As soon as Del saw them coming, he spun the wheel and the boat turned sharply, throwing Joe slightly off balance. This gave Mickey just enough time to draw his gun. He pointed it straight at Alicia.

"One more step and she's dead!" he said, grinning sadistically.

Mickey was watching Frank—not Alicia—and she used this time to drop down behind her stool. The few seconds it took for him to look her way and get her in his sights again was all the time Frank needed.

He kicked out sharply, his entire body horizontal to the deck. His body had become one long weapon. His foot landed against Mickey's gun hand with such force that the gun flew into one of the wheelhouse windows, cracking it in two. Mickey reeled backward, tripping over the stool. He crashed against the deck, his head hitting the hard wood floor.

In the meantime Del lashed out at Joe, who was momentarily distracted checking out Alicia. The pilot grabbed Joe's gun hand, and the two wrestled. Joe was as strong as his opponent, but Del was at home on the rocking boat, and that was all the advantage he needed. He jerked back on Joe's hand, sending Joe down. The gun went flying out the door and splashed overboard.

Mickey's gun had landed behind Del, and Frank had to get by him to retrieve it—he lurched forward. But with Joe down, Del had the seconds he needed to pull his own gun from inside his jacket.

Before Frank could reach him, Del had drawn a bead on Frank.

"Say goodbye!" Del cackled as he wrapped his finger tightly around the trigger.

Joe watched in horror as the would-be killer took deadly aim at Frank.

"Nooooo!" he yelled. But his cry was drowned out by the roar of an exploding bullet.

Chapter
12

THE GUN FLEW out of Del's hand. He grabbed
his hand in pain as Joe and Frank looked at
Alicia, still crouched behind the stool, with the
revolver grasped firmly in her hand.

"Where did you learn to shoot like that?"
Joe asked, flabbergasted.

"You don't think you and Frank were my
dad's *only* students, do you?" she asked, keeping a watchful eye on both Del and Mickey.
"I've won the Bermuda women's trap-shooting
championship two years in a row."

"That was as close as I ever want to
come—" Frank's face was just beginning to get
its color back. "I owe you, Alicia."

"Me, too," Joe chimed in.

"Don't mention it," she said to Frank,

slightly embarrassed. Then she grinned at Joe and said, "But from *you*—I might collect."

Frank picked up Mickey's gun, while Joe managed to shut off the engines. After Joe revived Mickey and bandaged Del's hand, he escorted the two downstairs and tied them up and laid them to rest beside their colleague.

"I'm sorry it's dark down here." Joe grinned at them. "But there's a cord, a socket, and a bulb around someplace." He locked the door with the key he had taken from Mickey, and they all went topside again.

Frank stretched his arms and took a deep breath. "It's good to be free and out in the fresh air."

"Yeah. And there's only one thing on my mind right now," he said as he looked at Alicia with a glint in his eyes.

"What's that?" she inquired.

"*Food!*" We haven't eaten since breakfast yesterday!"

"That's right. It's ten-thirty already. Why don't you two see if you can scrounge up some breakfast while I figure out how to get us home," Frank said.

"I'll take care of it," Alicia offered. "I've been on deck all morning while you two were penned up below." She smiled, then turned and went looking for the galley.

"I've figured out the rendezvous point,"

Frank said, once he had Joe's attention. "See this point, where our present course intersects the course we were on yesterday?" He pointed to a spot on one of the charts he found in the wheel house. "It's about four miles off the coast of Florida, somewhere up by Jacksonville."

Joe studied the map. "Kruger probably uses a local fishing boat or something to pick up the cards at sea. That way there's no chance for customs officials to find anything on a boat coming in directly from Bermuda."

"The data is probably sent to Bermuda directly on disk," Frank continued. "The Number File that was on the disk you found had only American spelling. I noticed that eye color was spelled c-o-l-o-r and not c-o-l-o-u-r, so the disk was probably made up in the states."

He stopped to gather his thoughts. "The credit cards must either be manufactured in Puerto Rico or stashed there after they're stolen. Then they're taken by boat to Bermuda. The disks are small enough to be sent by mail without arousing suspicion, but the credit-card blanks need to be hand-delivered. Otherwise, it would be too easy to trace where the packages come from or where they're going."

Joe nodded. "Then the operation in Bermuda only stamps the cards."

"And they put on the holograms."

"Then the *Sea Mist* takes the finished cards to another boat, which sails into U.S. territorial waters."

"Right." Frank agreed. "After that, the cards are distributed through a network of operatives." He shook his head. "There're so many links in this chain that it's no wonder the police can't get enough evidence to stop the scam."

Frank and Joe sat silently for a moment. They were pleased that they had finally figured out Kruger's operation and captured three of his henchmen. But they also knew their job was not done—they still had no hard evidence against Kruger.

Frank turned the boat around to head back to Bermuda. He radioed the Coast Guard and explained how he'd calculated the rendezvous point with the other ship. The Coast Guard said they'd meet the other ship and notify the Bermuda police that the brothers and Alicia were safe and were returning with three of Kruger's band.

With the current against them, the journey back was nearly three hours longer than the trip out. They took turns sleeping and keeping watch, so by the time they arrived back in Bermuda at six A.M. on Saturday, they all were relaxed and well rested. They were met in Hamilton by Chief Boulton.

"Nice work, boys," Boulton said. "When I got the call from the Coast Guard, I did some checking on the names you gave them. Since this Gus fellow has his official residence listed as Kruger's villa, we now have sufficient cause to examine those premises. I woke the judge and just got a warrant a few minutes ago."

"Can Joe and I come?" Frank asked.

"Certainly. Although you'll have to stay back. And we'll have to keep your weapons." The chief turned to Alicia, whom he had known for a long time. "I'll keep the gun as well, if you don't mind, Alicia. I'll return it to your dad when I see him."

"Where *is* he?" she asked, glancing around. She had expected he'd be there to greet them.

"I don't know," the chief replied. "We tried to call yesterday, but the line was dead. We sent a squad car out, but there was no sign of him. The officers left a note for him saying that you were all right and that he should contact me. But I haven't heard from him." Chief Boulton couldn't hide his concern.

"Then let me go with you to Kruger's," Alicia pleaded. She knew if her father had disappeared, Kruger was behind it. Chief Boulton gave his okay.

A procession of four cars and two motorcycles left for the Kruger estate. The Hardys and Alicia rode with the chief, but nobody said much. They were all thinking about Montague.

When they reached the villa, the officers surrounded the house while Frank, Joe, and Alicia waited in the car. Chief Boulton banged on the front door of the villa. When no one answered, he ordered his men to break down the door.

Chief Boulton and one officer carefully entered the villa as Joe, Frank, and Alicia watched from the car. Then the chief came outside again and waved for the three to join him. They ran quickly to the front door.

"The place is empty," the chief informed them. "And it doesn't look like its occupants are planning to return."

They entered the living room. Against the front wall stood a fireplace that looked as though it had never been used. There was furniture throughout the house and pictures were still hanging on the walls, yet the house seemed deserted. The closets were empty, desk drawers and file cabinets had been cleaned out.

By now Chief Boulton had ordered his men to search the house thoroughly. "We might as well head back," he said, purposely avoiding Alicia.

Suddenly one of the officers called from the kitchen. "Chief! Chief! Come quick!"

The four of them ran into the kitchen. They looked around to see what the officer had discovered, but nothing looked out of the ordinary. The policeman, a thin man not much older than the Hardys, stood in the middle of the room. Before the chief could ask, the officer said, "Listen. Listen carefully." They stood silently in the middle of the kitchen listening. Not a sound.

"Wait," the officer whispered, seeing that the chief was about to speak. The group stood motionless, and finally the silence was broken.

Thump—thump—thump! The sound was below them. It stopped, then started up again.

"It's almost directly below us," Joe said, dropping to his knees. He popped up, looking around the room. "Here, help me move the refrigerator," he said to Frank.

They slid the refrigerator out from its place against the wall and surveyed the area where it had been. All they found was a bare wall and floor. The knocking had stopped.

"There's a room under here," Joe insisted. "And there must be a way down." He walked over to the stove. "Come on, help me move this."

"A stove has all sorts of connections in the back," Chief Boulton said.

Joe hopped onto the countertop next to the stove, then peered behind it. "Not this one," he said. He turned on one of the gas knobs for a burner, but nothing happened. "This one's not connected to anything!"

The chief and his officer pulled out the stove, which revealed a trap door.

"This is it," said Joe, reaching for the handle.

"Just a minute," the officer said. "There's someone down there." He pulled his revolver and slowly opened the trap door, then he leaned over and peered down a short staircase leading into a shallow basement. "There's a light on," he whispered.

Chief Boulton stepped over to the opening. "All right, whoever's down there, come out quietly, there's no escape."

But instead of a voice, the response was the knocking again. "It's coming from under the stairway," the officer announced. He stole down the stairs cautiously, and then looked beneath them. "Chief! There's a man tied up down here!"

The group thundered downstairs until they reached the bound and gagged body. Alfred Montague was on his back against the wall and apparently had been banging his heels against the stairway.

"Dad!" Alicia cried out as soon as she recognized him. She pushed past the men and pulled the gag from her father's mouth.

"Alicia!" he exclaimed. "I thought Kruger had you!"

She summed up their adventure in less than four sentences, anxious to hear her father's story. "What happened to you? Are you all right?"

"Yes, I'm fine. A little stiff, and pretty hungry." As Montague spoke, the young officer cut off the ropes that bound him.

"Kruger became suspicious of me, especially after he found out you two were using my place as your base." He glanced at Frank and Joe. "After his men picked up you boys and Alicia, he paid me a visit to find out how much I knew—saying he would trade information for Alicia's life. He went through all my files and found papers linking me with British Intelligence. Then he really started questioning me. He knew we were closing in on him, but he wasn't sure just how close we were. But he realized it was time for him to clear out."

"Then what happened?" Joe asked, hardly giving Montague time for a breath.

The intelligence man walked around the small hidden basement, shaking his legs and stretching out his arms as he continued his story. "Kruger's men had all gone, though some fellow named Croaker came back later.

Anyway, Kruger and I were alone. I think he was used to having his men do all the dirty work, so he wasn't about to do away with me himself. And he didn't like the idea of killing a government man, even though it was probably he who ordered the hit on Conway. Besides, Kruger had nothing to gain by killing me—*he* knew that everything *I* knew was already on file with headquarters."

Montague was still pacing, rubbing the back of his neck and shoulders, his eyes fixed on the gray concrete floor. "He wasn't going to kill me, but he couldn't just leave me free. He had to keep me out of the way for a while. So he brought me to the villa here, tied me up, and stuck me down here in the basement. He figured I'd be found eventually, but not until he was long gone." He looked up at Alicia, then at Frank and Joe, and smiled proudly. "He never thought you'd turn the tables on the boat."

Joe grinned back. Then, anxious to learn more, he asked, "Did Kruger take all his equipment with him?"

"Ah, you haven't really *seen* this place yet." He led the group to a door opposite the stairs, then reached in the room and switched on a light before ushering the group in.

"Wow!" Joe blurted out. "Just look at this setup!" The room was filled with printing presses, stamping machines, sorting devices, computers, file cabinets, and loads of tools. "This is an entire credit-card factory!"

"And yet it took only two or three people to run the operation," Montague said. "Kruger, and his partner, Powers, handled the computer while a couple of goons operated the machinery."

"That would be Croaker and Gus," Joe offered. "They probably worked the machines and took some of the boat trips. Then he had two more delivery men, Del and Mickey, operating the boat. Them plus the U.S.–based crew." Joe was making a mental count as he spoke.

"Oh, I almost forgot," the chief broke in. "The U.S. Coast Guard picked up four men in a boat off Jacksonville. The FBI was afraid they wouldn't have any evidence against the men since you boys foiled the drop, but then they found three hundred thousand dollars in cash on board. Most of the bills were marked and came from a deal that went down between an undercover agent and two crooks involved in the distribution of the phony cards.

"The undercover man had bought some of the cards. The FBI decided not to arrest the crooks—there was a better chance of being led to the kingpin if they paid them off in marked bills and waited to see where the money showed up.''

"That means we have seven of the gang members so far,'' Frank calculated out loud.

"No, eight. We picked Powers up earlier today, and we're holding him," Boulton said.

"But what about Croaker and Kruger?" Frank asked.

"Goodness!" Montague exclaimed. "What time is it? And what day?"

"Saturday, exactly seven-fifty-two."

"A.M. or P.M.?"

"A.M."

Montague seemed agitated. He spoke rapidly. "How long did it take you to get here from the harbor?"

"About twenty minutes. Why?"

"Kruger told me he was going to take the *Bermuda Star* to New York. That's his main U.S. distribution point. Even if I was found before the ship left, Kruger knew I wouldn't say anything as long as his men had Alicia."

"When did the boat leave?" Chief Boulton asked.

"It hasn't yet," Montague said, rushing his words. "Kruger said the *Bermuda Star* leaves at eight o'clock this morning, in eight minutes."

Chapter

13

"CAN WE MAKE the ship on time?" Joe asked, concerned that they might lose their last chance to pick up Kruger.

"Not even if we raced the whole way," the chief said.

"Well, what about calling and holding the ship until we arrive?"

"No, the *Bermuda Star* always leaves on time. If anything out of the ordinary happens, it's likely to spook Kruger. If he panics and goes into hiding, it'll take that much longer to fish him out."

"Besides," Montague added, "it'll be better if we let Kruger think he's getting away. We know he's the top man in this credit card ring, and he'll be met by the head of the U.S. operation when the ship arrives in New York. We'd like to get our hands on the New York chieftain, too. Even with Kruger behind bars, the New York head could probably keep the distribution operation going for another six months.''

"Even though we found all the machinery and know how the whole operation works?'' Alicia asked.

"The machinery is replaceable,'' Chief Boulton said. "And the organization still has a large stockpile of illegal cards that haven't been used. The key is to arrest the leaders—none of the other gang members will be able to carry on the operation without them.''

"What if we just let Kruger leave and then notify the FBI to catch him when he arrives in New York?'' Alicia asked.

"No, that's too risky,'' Montague said. "You can be sure that anyone in the business of counterfeiting credit cards will have a forged passport as well. With a disguise and a name change, Kruger could walk right through customs.

"I think it's important for someone to take the cruise with Kruger. We can't take a chance on losing him.'' Montague shook his head.

"I have no jurisdiction outside of Bermuda,'' Chief Boulton reminded them. "That leaves it up to you lot.''

"I can go," Montague suggested, and nodded at Frank and Joe. "And so could the boys."

"And Alicia," Joe insisted. "We wouldn't be here now if it weren't for her."

Montague was concerned about letting his daughter accompany them on what could be a dangerous voyage. But finally he relented.

"We're losing precious time," Frank broke in. "How can we get on that boat?"

"I just thought of something," Chief Boulton broke in. "If we start right now, we can get to Hamilton before the pilot boat leaves. That's the boat that brings the pilot back to port once he has navigated the *Bermuda Star* into open waters. We can call ahead and arrange for you to get aboard. When the pilot transfers back onto the pilot boat—you can get on the *Star*."

"Sounds good." Montague nodded. "Now, what can we do about your appearances?" He looked at each of the three teens. At first Joe and Frank thought he was talking about some sort of disguise. But Alicia realized that her dad was referring to the clothes the three of them had had on for the past couple of days.

"I'll have one of the officers at the station pick up some supplies for you," Chief Boulton offered. "There are some shops right near the station. He'll meet us at the pilot boat."

"He'll need to hurry," Frank reminded him.

"And so will we!" Joe nodded at Frank, then turned and threw a quick wink at Alicia.

The group ran to the car. They raced back to town, sirens blasting, led by a motorcycle escort.

They arrived just in time to catch the pilot boat. The *Bermuda Star* was already in open water; the pilot was waiting to be picked up.

"I was just about to leave without you," the pilot boat captain said. He was an elderly man with a heavy gray beard and a heavier British accent. "But the officer here kept delaying me, insisting you wouldn't be but another minute." He was referring to one of Chief Boulton's men who stood next to the captain on the dock.

"I hope these things fit," the uniformed man said to Montague and the three youths. "I picked up a variety of loose-fitting clothes and some toilet articles. Anything else you need you should be able to buy on the boat." He handed them three large plastic bags. "I hope you'll find the things satisfactory, miss," he said to Alicia.

The figure of the policeman on the dock became smaller and smaller as the pilot boat bumped across the choppy waves of the harbor. They reached the *Bermuda Star* nearly two miles from port. The pilot climbed down before the four new passengers went up the ladder. The transfer was a bit difficult because of the wind that had come up forecasting a new storm. The three youths and Montague were happy to finally be on board. They were ready for a luxury cruise to New York.

"I'm glad there were a couple of cabins empty," Alicia said. "I'd hate to spend another night in the hold."

"And they're connecting cabins, too!" Joe had a twinkle in his eye as he looked at Alicia, then turned bright red as he remembered that Montague was there, watching and listening to it all.

"Let's get settled in our connecting cabins," Montague suggested with a grin. "We can change and freshen up."

"Then we'll have to go over the passenger list and see if we can spot Kruger."

"Remember, though," Frank cautioned, "we can't let Kruger spot us. He thinks we're dead, and if he knows we're on to him, he'll give us—and the police—the slip."

The four were led to their cabins on C-deck by a proper and polite purser who had been instructed to cooperate with them. Only the purser, the captain, the ship's doctor, and the ship's radio operator had any knowledge of the group's mission. The purser produced a map of the ship, announced he would be at their service should they require assistance, and returned to his office.

The two connecting cabins were near the end of a narrow corridor, slightly aft of the middle of the ship. Montague and Alicia took C-111, and the Hardys took C-112, which was closest to the door leading to the deck.

"I hate to stay cooped up," Joe said, complaining almost instantly. "Oh. We forgot to ask the purser for the passenger list."

"And—since there's no telephone service—*one* of us has to go to the purser's office to get the list," Frank said. "I wonder who should go?" he asked innocently. "Well, I guess it might as well be you, Joe, right?" he said, laughing. "Think you can make it there and back without wandering off in search of adventure?"

Joe opened the cabin door and checked the corridor before leaving the room. He hurried along the passageway, then proceeded cautiously toward the front of the ship and up to B-deck.

"There was no Kruger on the passenger manifest," the purser said. "So I have compiled a list. These are the men traveling without families who fit the description given us by the Hamilton police. There are eight names and room numbers."

"Thanks very much."

"One of the men—this one here," the purser said, pointing to a name on the list, "is in the dining room right now having breakfast; I saw him sit down a couple of minutes ago."

"Weisberg," Joe muttered, reading the name on the list. "I guess he's as good to start with as anyone. Can you point him out to me?"

Joe and the purser slowly made their way to the dining room. The boat was rolling more than usual—a storm was definitely going to kick up. "There," the purser said, nodding with his head. "The man eating alone."

Joe could see a partial profile of the diner's face. He had a full head of dark hair, glasses, and the beginnings of a beard. Joe remembered Kruger as clean-shaven and with gray hair and no glasses. This man didn't look like Kruger. But there was something familiar about him. Joe kept watching. Then the man turned to order something from the waitress, and Joe got a good look at his full face.

Bingo! It *is* Kruger! The eyes. Those were the same eyes, and they gave him away. "Yeah, that's him, all right! There's no way to disguise those eyes."

There was no doubt in Joe's mind that the man he was looking at was Kruger masquerading under the name of Weisberg. For the first time, it seemed, something was going right.

The first person on the list of possible Krugers was the head man himself.

"That's great," Joe said when they were back in the purser's office. "Thanks very much. If anything happens, we're in cabin C-one-twelve."

"Yes, I know," the purser said. "I have the passenger list, remember?" He paused long enough for a quick smile. "And the other gentleman, Mr. Weisberg, is in cabin B-thirteen on the deck above you—this deck—and farther forward."

Joe started back for his cabin. Kruger just sat down to eat, he thought to himself. So there's no way I could run into him if I went past his cabin. I'll just take the long way back to my cabin, get some fresh air.

He pushed hard against the door and went out on the deck. The wind was blowing hard, and the voyage was very rocky now. The passengers had already gone inside, and Joe found himself quite alone. He held on to the railing that ran along the side of B-deck beneath the lifeboats. He pulled himself forward and decided to go back in. There was a door. He staggered toward it and yanked on the handle. A burly man flew out and rammed right into him.

"Sorry," the man grumbled in a gravelly voice. He was stocky and muscular, dressed in a blue turtleneck. He looked up, then froze, glaring up into Joe's astonished face.

Joe had been so busy concentrating on Kruger that he had forgotten about Kruger's murderous henchman—Croaker!

Chapter

14

THE TWO OF THEM just stood there. Croaker thought Joe was dead—thrown overboard on the *Sea Mist*. And Joe had forgotten about Croaker. Now the two were face-to-face.

Croaker was stunned—unsure what move to make on a ship that offered no escape. He blocked the doorway with his stocky frame, preventing Joe from entering the passageway.

Joe stood fast. He controlled his first impulse to slug the crook. For all Joe knew, Croaker could be carrying a gun. And although the deck was empty for the moment, a passenger or ship's officer could walk by at any time.

"There's no way out of this one, Croaker," Joe told the thug. "No place to go." He paused, his tone and his stare unwavering. "Give yourself up."

Croaker's eyes never left Joe's. Without changing a wrinkle of his flat and fixed expression, he suddenly croaked, "Kid, you die!"

Joe wasn't ready for those words. He also wasn't ready when Croaker lunged at him, knocking him down onto the deck. Croaker started to pin him down, and Joe could feel the shape of a revolver as Croaker's chest pressed against his.

Joe struggled against the bulk of the muscular body. Croaker was strong, but Joe knew the thug wasn't as agile as he was. Wiggling like an eel, Joe managed to free one arm. He brought his fist down on the back of the stocky man's neck. The blow stunned Croaker just long enough for Joe to shift his body and push, toppling Croaker onto his side.

Another powerful shove and the thug went sprawling on the deck. Joe sprang up then and pounced. But as he landed, Croaker wasn't there. The ship, hit by a heavy wave, had heeled over, sending a salty spray over the two. Croaker had rolled away, and Joe missed. A second later Croaker was trying to pin him again.

The two of them rolled from side to side with the pitching and tossing of the ship. It seemed as though the fight was alternating between slow motion and fast forward. Balance was the key. And each time one had the advantage, the movement of the ocean liner upset that balance, and the other wound up on top.

Joe was on the bottom now. Croaker had one hand on Joe's throat; the other hand was trying to extract his gun. Joe's left hand was clawed into Croaker's face as Joe tried to push the powerful little man off him. Croaker's neck was bent back as Joe kept pushing with all his strength. But Croaker didn't budge. Joe's right hand was busy trying to tear Croaker's fingers from his neck.

Joe saw Croaker's right hand come out from under his jacket with a gun grasped tightly in his fingers. Joe couldn't loosen his opponent's grip on his throat, nor could he push him away.

Releasing his hold, Joe suddenly locked his fingers together behind Croaker's neck and yanked. Croaker's head was pulled sharply downward until the thug's skull smacked into Joe's.

The pain was excruciating for Joe, but much worse for Croaker. At least Joe was expecting it—and it was certainly less painful than a bullet would have been. Joe recovered faster than his rival, and in two quick moves was on top of him, holding Croaker's gun.

Again the ship rocked. Joe kept his balance, but Croaker smashed out with his left forearm, sending the revolver flying from Joe's hand. The gun skittered across the deck, under the bottom railing, and into the violent waters.

Joe slugged the squat man in the jaw. Then he got to his feet, his fingers clasped tightly around Croaker. Croaker rose, offering little resistance. They stood less than five feet from the railing, and Joe's head was about six inches from the bottom of the lifeboat which hung overhead.

Then the boat pitched again. Joe's head slammed against the lifeboat, his grip loosened, and the stocky man slid to the ground. The ship rolled, and Joe was tossed against the railing, with Croaker leaping at him.

Frank was beginning to worry what was keeping his brother. Suddenly, between the sounds of the crashing waves, he heard a shrieking cry.

"Man overboard! Man overboard!"

He rushed out of the cabin, down the passageway, around the corner, and onto the deck.

Once again the cry carried through the sea air. "Man overboard!" It was coming from the deck above. Frank staggered aft against the rocking motion to an outside stairway leading up to B-deck, then made his way back toward the center of the ship.

"Joe!" he cried out.

Joe was holding on to the railing under one of the lifeboats. Two ship's officers were moving toward the youth from the opposite direction. Frank reached his brother shortly after one of the officers. He caught the end of Joe's excited story.

"Then the ship rolled, he lost his balance, and went right overboard."

"What was he doing out here in this weather?" the first officer asked.

"I have no idea. I just opened that door there to have a look outside and breathe some fresh air, and I saw him by the railing. He went over before I could even call out." Joe extended his hand, which was clutched around a small brown wallet. "This fell out of his pocket."

As the officer took the wallet and opened it, Frank caught a glimpse of the picture on a photo ID. He tried not to show any surprise at seeing Croaker's face. He put his hand on his brother's shoulder, and waited until the officers left before he said anything.

The officer closed the wallet and looked again at Joe. "Who are you?"

"Joe Hardy. I'm in cabin C-one-twelve."

"We have to get to the bridge," the second officer interjected, "and get the ship turned around. We might need to talk with you again, later."

Joe nodded, then turned to his brother as the officers left.

"Croaker!" Frank exclaimed in astonishment.

"I bumped into him on deck, and—"

"Tell me inside," Frank interrupted. "It's really rough out here."

"Wait a minute," Joe said. He braced himself on the underside of the lifeboat. "Croaker decided to fight. He went down and hit his head against the railing there."

"And went *overboard?*"

"He was knocked cold. But his gun went overboard during the fight, and that gave me an idea." Joe climbed to the top of the lifeboat and started undoing the canvas cover. Frank stared at his brother's struggle to keep his footing for a second, then climbed up to help with the knots. "I realized if we held Croaker captive, Kruger would be tipped off about us as soon as he knew Croaker was missing. But if everyone thought that Croaker had gone overboard—"

He pulled off the cover to reveal Croaker lying unconscious in the bottom of the lifeboat. "This seemed like a better idea. Now, help me get him out."

Removing the unconscious Croaker from the lifeboat was not easy. Joe climbed in and handed the lifeless body down to Frank, all the while afraid that someone might walk out on the deck at any moment. But the rough weather let them work unobserved. Then the two brothers propped the thug between them, went inside, and walked him back to their cabin like two men escorting a drunken friend.

"This is incredible," Frank said when they got Croaker back to the cabin. "You've managed to get an entire ocean liner to turn around! The crew will be searching for a body that doesn't exist."

"There was nothing else I could do without spooking Kruger. Let's hope he doesn't think Croaker's accident was suspicious."

"We should tell Montague." Frank furrowed his brow as he stopped to think out their next move. "We'd better stay in the cabin and have Montague tell the captain what happened. Then he can arrange to have Croaker locked in the brig."

Frank knocked on the door adjoining the two cabins. A second knock brought Alicia to the door.

"This rocking put me right to sleep," she said. "But it's put Dad right out of commission." The Hardys peered in the other cabin and saw Montague lying in bed, a white washcloth splashed across his green face.

"That's too bad." Joe shook his head. Then he looked at Alicia. "We need you to do something for us." Joe described his encounter with Croaker briefly as he pressed a wet towel against his forehead. Alicia's pretty face had made him forget his aching head for a few seconds.

"What happened to your head, Joe!"

"Nothing." He winced. "I just bumped it."

Alicia looked over at Croaker, whom she recognized as one of her captors. She grinned, pleased that he was now the captive. "Funny, your friend here has a forehead as red as yours. Must be something going around."

"He's coming to," Frank observed. "You should go now, Alicia, and tell the captain."

Alicia left. The Hardys used a sheet torn into strips to tie their prisoner's hands behind his back, and when Croaker regained consciousness, they began questioning him.

"How many more of you are there?" Frank asked the stocky man.

"There's just me. My mother didn't want no more children," he answered.

"I can see why," Joe told him. "But I want to know about your gang. Are there any more of you on the ship besides you and Kruger?"

"Will I get a shorter sentence if I tell you?"

"Yeah," Joe said sarcastically. "We promise we won't use sentences with more than six words."

Croaker looked confused. "There's nobody on this boat except me and Kruger."

"And what cabin are you in?" Joe asked.

"The one next to Kruger."

"What *number?*"

"Uh, B-twelve." Croaker's voice was like short bursts of machine-gun fire. Frank kept wanting him to clear his throat, but it *was* clear.

"Did you charge things on my dad's credit card so we wouldn't be able to use it?" Joe asked, remembering the three thousand dollars the card was over the limit.

"Yeah. It was Kruger's idea—to slow you down."

"And how did Kruger—?" A knock on the door interrupted Frank's question. It was Alicia with the purser and a rather large seaman dressed in khakis and a sailor's cap.

"The captain is in my office explaining to your friend the circumstances under which his traveling companion went overboard." The purser spoke as though he were on the stage. "It would be best for us to remove this gentleman at the moment, while the other gentleman is occupied. That way we can ensure getting him down to the brig unnoticed."

"Great," said Joe.

"Now we're up to the hard part," Frank reminded them after the two crewmen left with the thug. "We've got to stay out of sight until we land. Then we've got to be right on top of Kruger when he makes his move."

"Oh, dear," Alicia said, like a heroine from an old movie. "And to think I'm practically confined to my cabin like a prisoner for two whole days with no one to talk to but a seasick father and you two boys!"

The two days went quickly, and once the storm subsided, it was a relaxing voyage. Joe enjoyed the time he spent with Alicia—even if they did have a chaperon. Montague felt better the second day of the voyage, and he shared adventure stories with the two detectives. And they weren't cooped up for the entire trip. The captain, the purser, and the ship's doctor advised the group of Kruger's whereabouts. When Kruger was eating, they found it possible to spend some time out on deck. Kruger, meanwhile, spent most of his time in his cabin. He seemed to accept the captain's story about "poor" Croaker.

By the time the ship docked in New York City, Kruger was visibly nervous—he'd have been more nervous if he knew what was waiting for him: Fenton Hardy and a host of federal agents. But Kruger was smart—and cool. When he walked off the ship into customs, he looked like any other passenger.

Fenton Hardy and the others—three under-cover feds—were stationed at different points in the large customs hall, past the customs checkpoint.

Joe stayed on board with Alicia, where he had a good view of the customs checkpoint set up on the dock below. Frank, meanwhile, fol-lowed Kruger, staying far back and out of sight.

Kruger, still in disguise and using a forged passport, passed through customs without any difficulty. He walked straight toward a tall, distinguished-looking gentleman in a gray suit, carrying an umbrella which he used as a cane. The New York ringleader lifted his head in a slow nod and proceeded into the large customs hall. Kruger followed him to the center of the large room. The head of the credit card scam in the United States and the chief of the coun-terfeiting operation in Bermuda shook hands, never suspecting that they were being ob-served.

Just then, a scratchy voice bellowed out above the din of the crowded customs hall: "Kruger, it's a trap! A trap!" It was Croaker, shouting from the side of the room. He was under the guard of two uniformed police offi-cers who were leading him through the large building. Though his movements were re-stricted, his grating voice was not. "Run for it!'' he shouted again before the officers could quiet him.

The distinguished-looking man lifted his umbrella like a sword and ran swiftly in the direction from which he had just come. Kruger froze, staring in the direction of Croaker.

Joe heard Croaker inside the shed and immediately swung into action. Literally. He leaped over the railing, grabbing on to one of the ship's mooring lines. Then he rode the cable down onto the dock below, avoiding the crowd that was choking the gangway. Landing squarely on two feet, he rushed toward the checkpoint.

In the crowded hall, a commotion erupted as the dapper man carved a path for himself with his umbrella. The two federal men pursued him, but their progress was hampered by the curious onlookers. The crook passed through the door leading out of the large room—only to be tackled some three feet later by Fenton Hardy.

Meanwhile, Bernhard Kruger, still cool and still composed and looking completely innocuous, turned, walked slowly, and disappeared into the crowd that had stopped to watch the spectacle.

Chapter
15

KRUGER'S NEW YORK CONTACT was in the hands of the police, but the big man himself was walking to freedom. Frank tried to race after him but was held back by the crowds.

Joe was stopped at the checkpoint by the customs officer on duty. Before he had a chance to explain, a blue-suited gentleman ran up, flashed a badge at the official, and motioned for Joe to go through.

Montague and Alicia were still on the ship, trying to push their way through the crowd. They were too far back to participate in the chase, but they wanted to get into the main terminal in case Kruger tried to outsmart his pursuers and double back.

Frank was rushing through the crowd, with

Joe not far behind. Every once in a while he thought he caught a glimpse of Kruger, but he couldn't be · sure. Still, there was only one direction the gang leader could have gone.

Frank ran through a large double door leading into the main terminal. The customs area seemed calm and orderly compared to the turmoil here. At least in customs everyone was moving in the same direction. Here people were coming and going, with patterns of cross-traffic merging and blocking the way.

Frank saw a couple of federal officers handcuffing the man with the umbrella. They were in a hallway. Kruger wouldn't have gone in their direction, Frank thought, turning toward the main exit.

Then he caught sight of Kruger. "Hold it!" His loud voice rose above the din of the crowded terminal. "The police have the exits covered."

Kruger peered over his shoulder at his pursuer. He knew he couldn't outrun the young detective, so he looked for the area with the most people. He turned right, away from the main exit, and darted down a corridor marked *Taxis/Buses*. Once again he disappeared into the crowd.

Frank ran as fast as he could without knocking anyone over. But there was no sign of the master criminal. Just when he thought he had lost Kruger for good, the counterfeiter came rushing out of the crowd—heading straight for him!

Frank was startled. He stood his ground, planting his feet firmly, wondering what the slick German was up to.

Then he saw it. Right behind Kruger was Fenton Hardy, running faster than Frank had ever seen him go. His father had a gun, and it seemed Kruger would rather face a youthful, unarmed athlete than a gun-toting private eye.

"I've got him, Dad!" Frank shouted, positioning himself in the middle of the corridor.

"Get out of the way, everyone!" Fenton ordered as he continued his pursuit.

The crowd thinned out, with people pinning themselves against the wall to avoid getting involved. Kruger knew he couldn't get past Frank, so he tried the next best thing—he ran smack *into* him!

Kruger was a heavy man, and he was in motion. There was no way Frank could brace himself. The impact knocked him off his feet. Kruger was down on one knee, but like a football player who doesn't believe the ball is dead, he scrambled up and continued his escape down the corridor.

Then he stopped short. Joe Hardy stood at the end of the corridor, blocking Kruger's avenue of escape, and he *was* braced and ready.

Kruger couldn't try the same trick again. But there was the crowd behind Joe. Fenton Hardy couldn't fire a gun where a bullet might hit an innocent passerby.

Kruger kept coming, passing a couple who had been on the boat and were now huddling against the wall. Sticking out of one of the bags they clutched were two bottles of duty-free rum. Kruger grabbed one of the bottles, smashing its bottom against the wall. He moved up the corridor toward Joe more slowly now, holding the broken bottle firmly by its neck. Then he whipped around as Frank came up behind him. The jagged edges of his bottle gleaming, Kruger pointed them at his challenger.

Frank backpedaled, whipping off the light windbreaker he had been wearing and wrapping it around his left arm. He was about four feet from Kruger now. The two began to circle around in the middle of the passageway, like two wrestlers preparing to get into a clinch.

"Give it up," Frank said, staring his opponent squarely in the eye.

"Never!" Kruger replied. "I have nothing to lose now—and *you're* responsible for everything I've lost already. You should be dead, and before they grab me, you will be."

Frank faked a charge to force Kruger into action. Kruger stepped back and to the side, then lunged at Frank with the broken bottle.

The sharp-edged glass ripped into Frank's jacket.

Kruger thrust again. This time Frank moved his arm quickly upward, and the bottle gouged out a piece of Frank's sleeve, coming close to his chest. Having drawn his opponent in toward him, Frank turned his left hand and grabbed Kruger's wrist. He pushed down on the man's hand, shoving the bottle away. Then, with his right hand, Frank delivered a mighty blow to Kruger's jaw, stunning him.

The bottle fell from Kruger's hand, crashing to the floor. Frank let go of his assailant's arm, wound up, and sent a smashing left hook into the side of Kruger's face, bringing the criminal to his knees. With both hands, Frank lifted him off the ground by his lapels. Kruger was beaten.

Frank was unhurt but winded. Joe and his father reached the fight from different directions at the same time, and Joe stepped in to put an armlock on Kruger while Frank unwound his windbreaker from his arm.

"Got you at last." Joe stopped as he saw Alicia and Montague running down the corridor, with two FBI men not far behind. He grinned when he saw Alicia's smile.

The Port Authority police and FBI took charge of the defeated criminal. They escorted him away in silence, leaving Fenton Hardy in charge of the rest of the group.

Frank and Joe turned to their dad. "Good to see you," they said.

"And you." The senior Hardy smiled. "So—how was Bermuda?"

Frank and Joe both laughed.

"Well, hello, Fenton." Montague beamed. And after a hearty handshake, he added, "This is Alicia."

"I've heard a lot about you," the elder Hardy said. Then he noticed the twinkle in Joe's eye as his young son gazed at this attractive girl. "And I guess I'll be hearing a lot more." Joe turned slightly red, and everyone laughed.

"I have a message for you from your pals," Frank told his sons. "Chet, Tony, and Biff are waiting at the pizza parlor. I think they ordered a pie with 'Welcome Home' written on it in anchovies."

"Sounds good to me," Frank said.

"Yeah. What do you say we get moving," Joe added.

"Wait a minute," Montague said. "There's the problem of Alicia."

"Alicia?"

"At first, immigration wouldn't let me off the ship," Alicia explained, "because I didn't bring a passport. In fact, I don't even have *any* identification—Kruger's men took everything I had. They let me through because of your father's reputation with the FBI. But we have to go back to immigration now in order for a U.S. citizen to take responsibility for me."

"Can you be put in *my* custody?" Joe asked, trying to keep a straight face.

"Never mind them," Fenton Hardy said through a smile. "I'll take care of everything."

"Oh, and there's one more thing," Montague interrupted with a more serious look on his face. "The FBI told me that Kruger and the New York head man are under indictment in the U.S. and will be arraigned here. But Croaker will have to be extradited back to Bermuda to stand trial along with Mickey, Gus, and Del."

"I hate to tell you this," Montague continued, trying to suppress a growing smile, "but it looks as if Joe and Frank are going to have to return to Bermuda in a few weeks to testify."

Frank gave a very loud—and phony—sigh.

Alicia broke into a big grin—and Joe blushed again.

"Well," Joe said as he took Alicia's arm, "these are the sacrifices a crack detective has to make."

Frank and Joe's next case:

Has Gertrude Hardy found true love at last? That's how it seems when Frank and Joe's aunt meets Cyril Bayard. Then the distinguished-looking stockbroker vanishes, along with Gertrude's life savings. When Bayard turns up dead, the Hardys' aunt becomes the number-one suspect.

Entering the shady underside of New York City's financial community, Frank and Joe must outmaneuver greedy Wall Street types. But someone is intent on eliminating the boys before they uncover the truth behind Bayard's death. The evidence that will reveal the killer's identity is hidden in a missing briefcase. Will the Hardy boys locate it in time to save Aunt Gertrude? Find out in *A Killing in the Market*, Case #18 in The Hardy Boys Casefiles™.